BEWARE! BEWARE!

Why didn't they come! There was a movement inside the house. Someone was coming to the door, but a man was coming up the path.

Susan banged louder, hoping that the noise would frighten him off. She realised that she was trapped between the man and whoever was about to open the door, and with all her might she willed it to be Mum or Dad. But then as Mum opened the door, it came to her beyond all shadow of doubt that although they still loved her as much as she loved them, Mum and Dad were DEAD . . .

BEWARE! BEWARE! is a collection of nine original chilling tales ready to thrill you.

BEWARE! BEWARE!

Chilling Tales

_____

compiled by
Jean Richardson

Hodder and Stoughton

First published in Great Britain in 1987 by Hamish Hamilton Children's Books
Lightning edition published 1989

British Library C.I.P.

Beware! Beware!
1. Children's ghost stories in English, 1945–   Anthologies
I. Richardson, Jean
823'.-1'08375[J]

ISBN 0 340 50096 4

Printed and bound in Great Britain for Hodder and Stoughton Paperbacks, a division of Hodder and Stoughton Ltd., Mill Road, Dunton Green, Sevenoaks, Kent TN13 2YA. (Editorial Office: 47 Bedford Square, London WC1B 3DP) by Cox & Wyman Ltd., Reading.

CONTENTS

'And all who heard should see them there,
And all should cry Beware! Beware!'

Kubla Khan, S. T. Coleridge

THE SPRING

Peter Dickinson

When Derek was seven Great-Aunt Tessa had died and there'd been a funeral party for all the relations. In the middle of it a woman with a face like a sick fish, some kind of cousin, had grabbed hold of Derek and half-talked to him and half-talked to another cousin over his head.

'That's a handsome young fellow, aren't you? (Just like poor old Charlie, that age.) So you're young Derek. How old would you be now, then? (The girls – that's one of them, there, in the green blouse – they're a lot bigger.) Bit of an afterthought, weren't you, Derek? Nice surprise for your mum and dad. (Meg had been meaning to go back to that job of hers, you know ...)'

And so on, just as if she'd been talking two languages, one he could understand and one he couldn't. Derek hadn't been surprised or shocked. In his heart he'd known all along.

It wasn't that anyone was unkind to him, or even uncaring. Of course his sisters sometimes called him a pest and told him to go away, but mostly the family included him in whatever they were doing and some-

1

times, not just on his birthday, did something they thought would amuse him. But even those times Derek knew in his heart that he wasn't really meant to be there. If he'd never been born – well, like the cousin said, Mum would have gone back to her job full-time, and five years earlier too, and she'd probably have got promoted so there'd have been more money for things. And better holidays, sooner. And more room in the house – Cindy was always whining about having to share with Fran ... It's funny to think about a world in which you've never existed, never been born. It would seem almost exactly the same to everyone else. They wouldn't miss you – there'd never have been anything for them to miss.

About four years after Great-Aunt Tessa's funeral Dad got a new job and the family moved south. That June Dad and Mum took Derek off to look at a lot of roses. They had their new garden to fill, and there was this famous collection of roses only nine miles away at Something Abbey, so they could go and see if there were ones they specially liked, and get their order in for next winter. Mum and Dad were nuts about gardens. The girls had ploys of their own but it was a tagging-along afternoon for Derek.

The roses grew in a big walled garden, hundreds and hundreds of them, all different, with labels. Mum and Dad stood in front of each bush in turn, cocking their heads and pursing their lips while they decided if they liked it. They'd smell a bloom or two, and then Mum would read the label and Dad would look it up in his book to see if it was disease-resistant; last of all, Mum might write its name in her notebook and they'd give it marks, out of six, like skating-judges, and move on. It took *hours*.

After a bit Mum remembered about Derek.

'Why don't you go down to the house and look at the river, darling? Don't fall in.'

'Got your watch?' said Dad. 'OK, back at the car-park, four-fifteen, sharp.'

He gave Derek 50p in case there were ice-creams anywhere and turned back to the roses.

The river was better than the roses, a bit. The lawn of the big house ran down and became its bank. It was as wide as a road, not very deep but clear, with dark green weed streaming in the current and trout some-times darting between. Derek found a twig and chucked it in, pacing beside it and timing its speed on his watch. He counted trout for a while, and then walking further along the river he came to a strange shallow stream which ran through the lawns, like a winding path, only water, just a few inches deep but rushing through its channel in quick ripples. Following it up he came to a sort of hole in the ground, with a fence round it. The hole had stone sides and was full of water. The water came rushing up from somewhere underground, almost as though it were boiling. It was very clear. You could see a long way down.

While Derek stood staring, a group of other visitors strolled up and one of them started reading from her guide book, gabbling and missing bits out.

' ... remarkable spring ... predates all the rest of the abbey ... no doubt why the monks settled here ... white chalk bowl fifteen feet across and twelve feet deep ... crystal clear water surges out at about two hundred gallons a minute ... always the same temperature, summer and winter ...'

'Magical, don't you think?' said another of the tourists.

She didn't mean it. 'Magical' was just a word to her. But yes, Derek thought, magical. Where does it come from? So close to the river, too, but it's got nothing to do with that. Perhaps it comes from another world.

He thought he'd only stood gazing for a short time, hypnotised by the rush of water welling and welling out of nowhere, but when he looked at his watch, it was ten past four. There was an ice-cream van, but Dad and Mum didn't get back to the car till almost twenty to five.

That night Derek dreamed about the spring. Nothing much happened in the dream, only he was standing beside it, looking down. It was night time, with a full moon, and he was waiting for the moon to be reflected from the rumpled water. Something would happen then. He woke before it happened, with his heart hammering. He was filled with a sort of dread, though the dream hadn't been a nightmare. The dread was sort of neutral, half-way between terror and glorious excitement.

The same dream happened the next night, and the next, and the next. When it woke him on the fifth night, he thought this is getting to be a nuisance.

He got out of bed and went to the window. It was a brilliant night, with a full moon high. He felt wide-awake. He turned from the window, meaning to get back into bed, but somehow found himself moving into his getting-up routine, taking his pyjamas off and pulling on his shirt. The moment he realised what he was doing he stopped himself, but then thought why not? It'd fix that dream, at least. He laughed silently to himself and finished dressing. Ten minutes later he was bicycling through the dark.

Derek knew the way to the abbey because Mum was no use at map-reading so that was something he did on car-journeys – a way of joining in. He thought he could do it in an hour and a quarter, so he'd be there a bit after one. He'd be pretty tired by the time he got back, but the roads were flat down here compared with York-shire. He'd left a note on the kitchen table saying 'Gone for a ride. Back for breakfast.' They'd think he'd just gone out for an early-morning spin – he was always first up. Nine miles there and nine back made eighteen. He'd done fifteen in one go last month. Shouldn't be too bad.

And in fact, although the night was still, he rode as

though there was a stiff breeze at his back, hardly getting tired at all. Late cars swished through the dark. He tried to think of a story in case anyone stopped and asked what he was doing – if a police-car came by, it certainly would – but no one did. He reached the abbey at ten past one. The gate was shut, of course. He hadn't even thought about getting in. There might be ivy, or something.

He found some a bit back along the way he'd come, but it wasn't strong or thick enough to climb. Still, it didn't cross his mind he wouldn't get in. He was going to. There would be a way.

The wall turned away from the road beside the garden of another house. Derek wheeled his bike through the gate and pushed it in among some bushes, then followed the wall back through the garden. No light shone from the house. Nobody stirred. He followed the wall of the abbey grounds along towards the back of the garden. He thought he could hear the river rustling beyond. The moonlight was very bright, casting shadows so black they looked solid. The garden became an orchard, heavy old trees, their leafy branches blotting out the moon, but with a clear space further on. Ducking beneath the branches he headed towards it. The night air smelt of something new, sweetish, familiar – fresh-cut sawdust. When he reached the clear space, he found it surrounded a tree-trunk which had had all its branches cut off and just stood there like a twisted arm sticking out of the ground. Leaning against it was a ladder.

It wasn't very heavy. Derek carried it over to the abbey wall. It reached almost to the top. He climbed, straddled the wall, leaned down, and with an effort hauled the ladder up and lowered it on the further side, down into the darkness under the trees that grew there, then climbed down and groped his way out towards where the moonlight gleamed between the tree-trunks. Out in the open on the upper slope of lawn he got his bearings, checked for a landmark so that he would be able to find his way back to the ladder, and walked down in the shadow of the trees towards the river. His heart was beginning to thump, the way it did in the dream. The same dread, between terror and glory, seemed to bubble up inside him.

When he was level with the spring he walked across the open and stood by the low fence, gazing down at the troubled water. It looked very black, and in this light he couldn't see into it at all. He tried to find the exact place he had stood in the dream, and waited. A narrow rim of moon-shadow cast by the wall on the left side edged the disc of water below. It thinned and thinned as the slow-moving moon heeled west. And now it was gone.

The reflection of the moon, broken and scattered by the endlessly upswelling water, began to pass glimmeringly across the disc below. Derek could feel the turn of the world making it move like that. His heartbeat came in hard pulses, seeming to shake his body. Without knowing what he was doing, he climbed the fence and clung to its inner side so that he could gaze straight down into the water. His own reflection, broken by the ripples, was a squat black shape against the silver moonlight. He crouched with his left arm clutching the lowest rail and with his right arm strained down towards it. He could just reach. The black shape changed as the reflection of his arm came to meet it. The water was only water to his touch.

Somehow he found another three inches of stretch and plunged his hand through the surface. The water was still water, but then another hand gripped his.

He almost lost his balance and fell, but the other hand didn't try to pull him in. It didn't let go either. When Derek tried to pull free the hand came with him, and an arm behind it. He pulled, heaved, strained. A head broke the surface. Another arm reached up and gripped the top of the side wall. Now Derek could straighten and take a fresh hold higher up the fence. And now the stranger could climb out, gasping and panting, over the fence and stand on the moonlit lawn beside him. He was a boy about Derek's own age, wearing ordinary clothes like Derek's. They were dry to the touch.

'I thought you weren't coming,' said the boy. 'Have we got somewhere to live?'

'I suppose you'd better come home.'

They walked together towards the trees.

'Who ... ?' began Derek.

'Not now,' said the stranger.

They stole on in silence. We'll have to walk the whole way home, thought Derek. Mightn't get in before breakfast. How'm I going to explain?

The ladder was still against the wall. They climbed it, straddled the top, lowered the ladder the far side and climbed down, propping it back against its tree. Then back towards the road.

There were two bikes hidden in the bushes.

'How on ... ?' began Derek.

'Not now,' said the stranger.

They biked in silence the whole way home, getting in just as the sky was turning grey. They took off their shoes and tip-toed up the stairs. Derek was so tired he couldn't remember going to bed.

They were woken by Cindy's call outside the door.

'Hi! Pests! Get up! School bus in twenty mins!'

Derek scrambled into his clothes and just beat David down the stairs. Dad was in the hallway, looking through the post before driving off to work.

'Morning, twins,' he said. 'Decided to have a lie-in?'

They gobbled their breakfast and caught the bus by running. Jimmy Grove had kept two seats for them. He always did.

Very occasionally during that year Derek felt strange.

There was something not quite right in the world, something out of balance, some shadow. It was like that feeling you have when you think you've glimpsed something out of the corner of your eye but when you turn your head it isn't there. Once or twice it was so strong he almost said something. One evening, for instance, he and David were sitting either side of Mum while she leafed through an old photograph album. They laughed or groaned at pictures of themselves as babies, or in fancy dress – Tweedledum and Tweedledee – and then Mum pointed at a picture of an old woman with a crooked grinning face, like a jolly witch, and said, 'I don't suppose you remember her. That's Great-Aunt Tessa. You went to her funeral.'

'I remember the funeral,' said David. 'There was a grisly sort of cousin who grabbed us and told us how handsome we were, and then talked over our heads about us to someone else as if we couldn't understand what she was saying.'

'She had a face like a sick fish,' said Derek.

'Oh, Cousin Vi. She's a pain in the neck. She ... '

And Mum rattled on about Cousin Vi's murky doings for a bit and then turned the page, but for a moment Derek felt that he had almost grasped the missing whatever-it-was, almost turned his head quick enough to see something before it vanished. No.

On the whole it was a pretty good year. There were dud bits. David broke a leg in the Christmas hols, which spoilt things for a while. The girls kept complaining that the house wasn't big enough for seven, especially with the pests growing so fast, but then Jackie got a job and went to live with friends in a flat in Totton. Dad bought a new car. Those were the most exciting things that happened, so it was a nothing-much year, but not bad. And then one week-end in June Mum and Dad went off to the abbey to look at the roses again. Cindy and Fran were seeing friends, so it was just the twins who tagged along.

The roses were the same as last year, and Mum and Dad slower than ever, so after a bit David said, 'Let's go and look at the river. OK, Mum?'

Dad gave them a quid for ices and told them when to be back at the car. They raced twigs on the river, tried to spot the largest trout, and then found the stream that ran through the lawn and followed it up to the spring. They stood staring at the uprushing water for a long while, not saying anything. In the end Derek looked at his watch, saw it was almost four, woke David from his trance and raced him off to look for ices.

A few nights later Derek woke with his heart pounding. It was something he'd dreamt, but he couldn't remember the dream. He sat up and saw that David's bed was empty. When he got up and put his hand between the sheets, they were still just warm to the touch.

All at once memory came back, the eleven years when he'd been on his own and the year when he'd had David. The other years, the ones when he'd been growing up with a twin brother and the photographs in the album had been taken – they weren't real. By morning he wouldn't remember them. By morning he wouldn't remember David either. There was just this one night.

He rushed into his clothes, crept down the stairs and out. The door was unlocked. David's bike was already gone from the shed. He got his own out and started off.

The night was still, but he felt as though he had an intangible wind in his face. Every pedal-stroke was an effort. He put his head down and rode on. Normally, he knew, he'd be faster than David, whose leg still wasn't properly strong after his accident, but tonight he guessed David would have the spirit wind behind him, the wind from some other world. Derek didn't think he would catch him. All he knew was that he had to try.

In fact he almost ran into him, about two miles from the abbey, just after the turn off the main road. David was trotting along beside his bike, pushing it, gasping for breath.

'What's happened?' said Derek.

'Got a puncture. Lend me yours. I'll be too late.'

'Get up behind. We'll need us both to climb the wall. There mayn't be a ladder this time.'

Without a word David climbed onto the saddle. Derek stood on the pedals and drove the bike on through the dark. They leaned the bike against the wall where the ivy grew. It still wasn't thick enough to climb, but it was something to get a bit of a grip on. David stood on the saddle of the bike. Derek put his hands under his heels and heaved him up, grunting with the effort, till David could grip the coping of the wall. He still couldn't pull himself right up, but he found a bit of a foothold in the ivy and hung there while Derek climbed onto the cross-bar, steadied himself, and let David use his shoulder as a step. A heave, a scrabble, and he was on the wall.

Derek stood on the saddle and reached up. He couldn't look, but felt David reach down to touch his hand, perhaps just to say good-bye. Derek gripped the hand and held. David heaved. Scrabbling and stretching, Derek leaped for the coping. He heard the bike clatter away beneath him. David's other hand grabbed his collar. He had an elbow on the coping, and now a knee, and he was up.

'Thanks,' he muttered.

The drop on the far side was into blackness. There could have been anything below, but there seemed no help for it. You just had to hang from the coping, let go and trust to luck. Derek landed on softness but wasn't ready for the impact and stumbled, banging his head against the wall. He sat down, his whole skull filled with the pain of it. Dimly he heard a sort of crash, and as the pain seeped away worked out that David must have fallen into a bush. More cracks and rustles as David struggled free.

'Are you OK?' came his voice.

'Think so. Hit my head.'

'Where are you?'

'I'm OK. Let's get on.'

They struggled out through a sort of shrubbery, making enough noise, it seemed, to wake all Hampshire. Derek's head was just sore on the outside now. Blood was running down his cheek. David was already running, a dark limping shape about twenty yards away. His leg must have gone duff again after all that effort. Derek followed him across the moonlit slopes and levels. They made no effort to hide. If anyone had been watching from the house they must have seen them, the moonlight was so strong. At last they stood panting by the fence of the spring. The rim of shadow still made a thin line under a wall.

'Done it,' whispered David. 'I thought I was stuck.'

'What'd have happened?'

'Don't know.'

'What's it like ... the other side?'

'Different. Shh.'

The shadow vanished and the reflection of the moon moved onto the troubled disc. Derek glanced sideways at his brother's face. The rippled, reflected light glimmered across it, making it very strange, grey-white like a mushroom, and changing all the time as the ripples changed, as if it wasn't even sure of its own proper shape.

David climbed the fence, grasped the bottom rail and lowered his legs into the water. Derek climbed too, gripped David's hand and crouched to lower his brother – yes, his brother still – his last yard in this world. David let go of the rail and dropped. Derek gripped his hand all the way to the water.

As he felt that silvery touch the movement stopped, and they hung there, either side of the rippled mirror. David didn't seem to want to let go, either.

Different? thought Derek. Different how?

The hand wriggled, impatient. Something must be happening the other side. No time to make up his mind. He let go of the rail.

In the instant that he plunged towards the water he felt a sort of movement around him, very slight, but clear. It was the whole world closing in, filling the gap where he had been. In that instant, he realised everything changed. Jackie would still be at home, Fran would be asleep in his room, not needing to share with Cindy. Nobody would shout at him to come to breakfast. His parents would go about their day with no sense of loss; Jimmy Grove would keep no place for him on the school bus; Mum would be a director of her company, with a car of her own ... and all the photographs in the albums would show the same cheerful family, two parents, three daughters, no gap, not even the faintest shadow that might once have been Derek.

He was leaving a world where he had never been born.

WE'LL MEET AGAIN...

Adèle Geras

'Fan-tastic!' Maddy said, as she peered short-sightedly into a mirror that was, as she put it, 'more spots than silver'. She was wearing a brown felt hat and a brown woollen coat, with a fitted waist and a skirt that nearly touched the ground. 'This'll be more your size, Celia. You'd better try it on.' She took the coat off. 'Wherever did you get all this stuff? It's really amazing. I mean, it looks authentic.'

'It is authentic.' Celia was pulling the brown coat on. 'Honestly, Maddy, can't you do something about the mirrors? It's difficult to see what you look like ... what kind of shop is this, anyway?'

'It's not a shop. Hadn't you noticed? Just an oversized box full of second-hand clothes. My customers are used to it. If they want mirrors, they can go to Jaeger or Next or somewhere. Cheapo style, that's what I'm about. These are great, honestly. Forties is all the rage. You said they were authentic. Where did you find them?'

'I was given them. A man in our street let me take them. He was clearing up after his wife died.' Celia

13

paused. 'She died about two years ago, actually. I think he couldn't bring himself to clear up her stuff, and get rid of it ... not for ages ... anyway, when I got there, it was all ready in that box.'

'Dead sad, really,' said Maddy, 'when you think of it. Did you know her? The wife?'

'Well,' said Celia, 'by sight, you know. Not to talk to, not properly. My mum used to go in there and have a chat now and then. She was fat ... not very pretty. Not when I knew her ... '

Maddy had stopped listening and gone to lure a couple of helpless-looking people into her clothes-box. Celia stood in front of the mirror and tried to see herself in what little light there was. I look good, she thought. It suits me. Mrs Stockton was skinny like me, back in the forties. He said so. I wonder how much Maddy'll want for it.

Mr Stockton had been standing by the sideboard when she went in. 'Just a few things belonging to Irene,' he said, and twisted his head round as if he didn't want to look at anything, not at her and not at the clothes. 'They're no good to me now.' That's what he'd said, and then he'd laughed. 'Not much good to Irene either for a long time. She got too big for them in the end. There was a time,' he'd rubbed a clenched fist along the edge of his chin, 'when I could have put both my hands in a circle round her waist. She wasn't any thicker than you are now, a slip of a thing, was my Irene ... ' His throat had filled up then, like someone with a chesty cough. She thought he was having a hard job keeping himself from bursting into tears.

She'd said quickly, 'My friend Maddy'll like these. She's got a kind of stall in Affleck's Palace.' He didn't know about the Palace. She'd told him: 'It's where you go in Manchester for good, exciting, second-hand stuff. Is it all right? Taking it there?'

He nodded then. 'Yes, Irene was fond of young people ... would like to think of them enjoying her clothes.

You should try some,' he'd said, 'you're the right size ... '

'Oh, I couldn't,' she'd said, and now here she was in Irene's coat, and he was right. It was beautiful. Anyway, then she couldn't think of anything else to say, so she'd picked up the box. Looking back, she could see him standing in the window, stroking the back of his hand along his jawline.

'That looks great,' said Maddy, when the customers had gone. 'You should keep it.'

'How much do you want for it?'

'I'll let you have it for nothing. A kind of commission for bringing this treasure to me, and not trying to flog it to anyone else. You can have a dress too. There's got to be something ... ' She started rummaging about in the cardboard box. 'Here you go.' She held out a soft, slippery bit of what looked like nothing very much. 'Try that on.'

Celia went into the small space behind the bit-of-fabric-on-a-string that served Maddy as a fitting room. This isn't like me, she thought. These aren't my type of clothes at all.

Almost as though she had overheard Celia's thoughts, Maddy spoke from behind the curtain.

'I know it's not your type of gear, Celia, not really, but you should think about it seriously. I mean, that forties look really does something for you. You can wear that dress to the Forties Night next month.'

'What Forties Night?' Celia said, pulling the curtain back.

'Wowee!' Maddy shrieked. 'You look like a film star from one of those old black and white thingies ... What do you mean, what Forties Night? Every few months they have one ... down at the Ritz. Everyone dresses up and the music is Glenn Miller and stuff like that. It's great ... you must come, Celia. Promise you'll come.'

'Not got anyone to come with, have I?' Celia said, pulling the curtain across again. 'Still, I like the dress.

I'll have that, and thanks a lot.'

'Don't mention it,' said Maddy. 'And you don't need
to have a partner. You can come with me and Graham.'

Celia muttered something about gooseberries as the
dress came up over her head.

'You'll meet someone there,' Maddy said. 'Do say
you'll come. Go on ... you've got such a perfect outfit,
that dress in this wonderful slippery material with
those lovely blue leafy patterns all over it ... and the
coat on top of course. Please, Celia.'

'Right,' said Celia. 'I'll come. I'll probably regret it,
but I'll come.'

'Terrific,' said Maddy. 'Just for that, I'll let you take
your things home in a carrier bag. It's not every cus-
tomer who gets one of those, I can tell you!'

Later that same day, Celia struggled up the sloping
pavement to the station, wishing the books she had to
carry to college were lighter, wishing that Maddy's
carrier bag had a decent handle, one that didn't cut
your fingers as you held it. She was wearing the brown
woollen coat and had put her anorak into the bag, but
it didn't make it much lighter. She stood on the platform
waiting for the train to Birchwood, watching the dusk
wrap itself, mauve and grey and pink, around buildings
which suddenly looked soft at the edges. Only October,
she thought, and the evenings are coming earlier and
earlier.

When the train pulled in, she opened one of the doors
and then stood aside to let a weary-looking woman
hung about with a folding pushchair, crying baby and
assorted bits of shopping, get on before her. Celia
slammed the door shut and looked out of the window
as the train slowly slid away from the station. Someone
was standing on the platform, waiting, looking up and
down the line, as if expecting to see someone ... Celia,
who wasn't looking carefully, caught only a glimpse,
and by the time she looked back, the figure had shrunk

to almost nothing, but it seemed to her that the woman was wearing a brown coat very like hers. She was still peering up and down the platform, up and down ... Oh well, Celia said to herself, Maddy said forties styles were in. They must be more in than she thought. I'd better find somewhere to sit.

She sat down in the first seat she could find. It wasn't a non-smoking compartment, but it was only a ten-minute journey. I'm exhausted, Celia thought. She closed her eyes for a moment, thinking about the silky dress, dazzled for a second by a daydream of herself wearing it under one of those glass balls they had in dance halls, the kind that bounced darts of coloured light around the walls and on to the skin and hair of all the dancers ... She opened her eyes.

'Do you mind if I smoke?' said the young man who was now sitting opposite her.

'No ... not at all,' Celia said. Where on earth had he come from? How long, she wondered, have I been sitting here with my eyes closed? She glanced down at her watch – only a minute or so. He must have slipped in quietly. He's very polite. Fancy asking if I minded him smoking. Celia looked at him as he turned his head to look out of the window. Some kind of a soldier ... some sort of uniform ... very fair hair (dyed? thought Celia. You never knew, nowadays) but dark eyes ... maybe blue, but dark. A parting in the hair ... short at the back and sides and floppy at the front. As the train came into Birchwood, the young soldier stood up and smiled at Celia.

'Cheerio,' he said, and turned and walked down the compartment towards the door.

'Bye,' Celia said, still a little faint from the feelings brought on by that smile. I can't run after him, she thought. I'll use the other door. She jumped on to the platform and looked for him ... there he was, already over the bridge and on the other side. I should go after him, she thought. Call out to him. Being dignified and ladylike doesn't matter any more. What if I never see him again?

'Stop it!' Celia said aloud to herself, and then turned round to make sure she was alone. As she trudged over the bridge to where her father was waiting for her in the car, she told herself over and over again that she had only seen him for a few moments, that she would probably never see him again, and that she was being a fool. Nevertheless, she knew what it felt like to fall in love. It was as unmistakable as getting a cold, and she recognised within herself all the symptoms. The pain she felt at the very idea of never seeing him again made her want to cry. The headlights of her parents' car broke into a thousand small fragments of light in the tears she hadn't quite managed to blink away.

'I saw you on the train the other day, didn't I?'

'Yes, you asked if you could smoke,' Celia said. (Oh, glory be, here he is again ... ten whole minutes ... please, God, let the time go slowly ... slow it down ... let him like me ... thank goodness I'm wearing the brown coat.)

'Well,' said the soldier, 'it's only polite to ask. I should introduce myself. My name's Neville ... '

'Mine's Celia.'

'Delighted to meet you.'

What a funny way he has of talking, Celia thought. No one has ever said that to me ... delighted to meet you.

'Do you live in Birchwood?'

'I do at the moment, of course,' Neville said. 'Based there, you know. Training.'

'Training for what?'

'Army, of course. Lots of chaps training up here, now.'

'Oh.' Celia was silent, racking her brains. She'd never seen any soldiers around Birchwood – she would certainly have noticed – but then, she'd only lived there a short time. Perhaps it was possible – maybe even a highly secret camp that no one was supposed to know about. Celia was bored by military matters and thought of a way to change the subject.

'Are you meeting someone in Manchester?' she asked.

'Yes, as a matter of fact. It's ... well, it's a young lady.'

Neville blushed. Celia stared at him. She hardly knew anyone who blushed like that. She sighed. That's that, she thought. He's got a girl friend. Wouldn't you know it? First time for six months I meet a decent bloke and someone else has got there first.

'Perhaps I'll see you again ... ' he said.

'Yeah,' Celia said. 'Bye.'

She muttered to herself as she walked towards the barrier: 'Forget him ... forget him ... he'll never be for you ... he loves someone else.' As she left the station, she looked back towards the platform. Neville was still there, waiting. Hope she never shows up, Celia thought. Hope she's run away to Brazil with a second-hand car dealer. Hope she never comes back. I'll take care of Neville.

Celia looked at the lines of rain slanting across the window. Was that the same young woman, still waiting for someone? She was standing on the platform, waiting, but it was hard to see, through all that rain, who it was ... The train pulled out of the station.

'It's Celia, isn't it?' A voice interrupted her thoughts.

'Hello, Mr Stockton. Fancy seeing you here.'

'It's a bit late for you, young lady, isn't it?'

'Not really. I often go home on this train after a film or something – Mum or Dad meet me. We'll give you a lift as well.'

'That'll be grand.' Mr Stockton sighed. 'On a night like this.'

Celia said: 'Those clothes you gave me ... I hope you

19

don't mind. I kept a coat and dress.'

Mr Stockton looked at Celia out of dark eyes.

'Mind, child? I'm delighted. Irene would have been delighted. She did think a lot of you, I know that. A properly brought-up child she said, not like some. And I'm glad someone young'll be wearing her things again. You look a little like her ... she was thin ... had the same colour hair, too. Fine, like a baby's it was – that soft. Eeh, I wish I had a pound for every time I've been up and down to Manchester on this line. I did my training up at Birchwood during the War, like many others, you know ... oh yes ... and backwards and fowards I used to go, to meet Irene in Manchester.'

'Did you go dancing?'

Mr Stockton chuckled. 'Yes, dancing, and to the cinema, and did a bit of spooning too ... ' He sighed. 'Same as you get up to with your young man, I've no doubt.'

'I haven't got a young man,' Celia said.

'You will have,' Mr Stockton said. 'There's no rush.'

Celia opened her mouth to tell him about Neville, then changed her mind.

'Nearly home now,' said Mr Stockton. 'There was a time when it was all aircraft noises round here. In the War.'

'You look ... different tonight,' said Neville. 'I mean you look very smart, of course, and you remind me ... '

'Yes?' Celia asked.

'Well, you remind me of someone.'

'Is it your friend? The young lady you're always going to meet?' Celia was dressed up for Forties Night at the Ritz in the silky dress and the brown woollen coat.

'Yes – yes, you look very much like her. Especially now. Have I told you that before?'

'Once or twice.'

Neville looked away.

'I'm sorry. You see, it's not that I don't ... like you.
I like you most awfully – I mean I *could* like you, but I
have promised her ... '

'But you say she's never there. Never at the station
where she said she was going to be.' Celia's voice was
full of anger. 'I hate to say this, but I think she's gone
off you. I do really. Otherwise, why doesn't she turn up,
eh? Honestly, Neville, face the facts. Please.'

The train was slowing down. The lights of the platform slipped past the window like bright beads. Celia
stood up and Neville followed her.

'Celia!' Neville put out a hand, touched her sleeve.

'Yes?'

'You don't understand ... I have to meet her . . . she's
waiting for me ... it's just that I have to find her ... you
can't possibly understand.'

'Don't talk about understanding,' Celia shouted. 'I'm
fed up with it. Damn it, where's all your fine understanding? Can't you see that I love you? What do I have
to do? Walk around with a sign on?'

Neville took Celia's face in his hands and kissed her
softly on the mouth, so softly that she hardly felt it,
and yet a shiver ran through her as if his lips had been
ice-cold.

'I didn't know,' he said. 'I'm sorry. But I have to wait
for her. I didn't know.'

The train stopped. Celia tore the door open, jumped
out and ran towards the barrier. Through a fog of tears
she could see Maddy.

'What's your rush?' Maddy said. 'You look as if you're
running to save your life.'

'It's Neville. I'm fed up with him.'

'Ah, the mysterious unknown soldier. Let's get a
squint at him. Where is he?'

'Up there, probably. That's where he usually is.
Hanging about. Waiting for her.'

'Can't see a thing. Not a handsome soldier in sight
anywhere. Come on, chuck, let's go and rustle up some

grub, and then hit the Ritz with everything we've got.'

Maddy shimmied down the hill towards Oxford Road singing, asking innocent passers-by whether this was, indeed, the Chattanooga Choo-Choo. Celia followed her, stiff with misery.

'It isn't that bad, is it?' asked Maddy.

'It's terrible. All those people sweating, and everybody looking so – so ... '

'So what?'

Celia sighed. 'So fleshy. So ... ' She could find no words.

Maddy put an arm around her shoulders. 'You don't mean any of that. You mean, they aren't this Neville of yours.'

'He's not "mine,"' Celia said, 'He's someone else's. I'm sorry, Maddy. I'm going home. You and Graham stay. I'll be OK. Station's only across the road. Can you phone my mum and tell her I'm on the eleven-eighteen? I don't feel like talking to her ... and I can't stand the music, Maddy, and that's the truth.'

'What's the matter with it? It's great.'

'It makes me feel like crying. All that stuff about not knowing where and not knowing when, and the blue skies driving the dark clouds far away. I've never really thought before, what it must have been like ...' she paused, 'to be in love with someone who could die at any moment, and to be in danger yourself.'

'Go home,' said Maddy. 'I can see what kind of mood you're in. And Graham's walking you up the hill, and I don't care what you say.'

'I'll go and get my coat,' Celia said.

Celia huddled against one of the pillars, trying not to be seen. The clock on the platform said eleven-fifteen. Three more minutes ... oh, please, please, she thought, make him not look up. Make him not see me. She bit her lip and felt hope, any hope she had at all, drain out of every bit of her. Across the other platform she could see them quite clearly, standing under one of the lights. They stood close together. He had found her at last, his girl, the one he had been coming to meet all those other times. He was looking down at her – she seemed to fit herself into the circle of his arm, khaki against the brown fabric of her coat ... A coat a lot like this, Celia thought, and glanced at them again. They had turned to leave now. Neville still had his arm fixed around the woman. It seemed to Celia that his arm was fixed there forever, that nothing could move it. At the barrier they stopped, and the woman stood on tiptoe so that he could kiss her. Celia watched them and felt sick. Where the hell was the train? She began to cry as it came into the station.

'Lovey,' said Celia's mother, 'what is it? What's happened? You surely can't have heard ... '

'No, I'm fine ... really ... I just ... it doesn't matter. Heard what?'

'About poor old Mr Stockton.'

'What about him?'

'He died. Just about half an hour ago, that's all.'

'How do you know?'

'Betty told me. She heard a crash. He pulled an armchair over as he fell. It was very quick. He can't have felt any pain. Poor thing! I feel sad. He hasn't any children or close family that we know of. I'll have to go over there and help Betty pack up his stuff. Tomorrow probably, or the next day. D'you want to give me a hand, love?'

'Might as well,' said Celia. I don't think I'll ever care strongly about anything ever again, she thought. My whole body feels like a mouth does after an injection at the dentist's. Numb, but with layers of pain hidden away, hidden deep down and far away.

The darkness makes you silly, Celia thought the next

day. She and her mother and Betty, Mr Stockton's next door neighbour, were packing the old man's life away in cardboard boxes. Yesterday he was here, and now he isn't, she said to herself. Yesterday, when Neville kissed me in the corridor of the train, I thought there was a chance, a hope of something, and now I know there isn't. I should be able to pack the remains of what I feel into a box and give it to Oxfam. Get rid of it.

'How are you getting on?' Celia's mother shouted from the kitchen.

'Fine,' Celia yelled back. 'Just doing these albums ...'

'Having a peep, are you?' Celia's mother came into the room.

'Can't help it. I'm nosey and I love all these old brown photos ... only some of them are so small, you can hardly see what anybody looks like.'

'There's one fallen out, Celia. Be careful.'

Celia's mother bent to pick up the photograph. She smiled.

'This is a bit more like it. A bit bigger. Goodness, look at Irene Stockton on her wedding day! During the War, it must have been ... he's in uniform. Registry Office wedding, of course ... look how thin and pretty she was, and as for him, well, you'd never believe it was the same person as our Mr Stockton. Here, take it and push it in somewhere. I've got to get back to the kitchen ...' Celia's mother left the room.

Celia sat looking at the photograph for a long time, and allowed herself to cry. Not for Mr Stockton, who had found his Irene at last, pretty in her silky, leaf-strewn dress and brown woollen coat, nor for Neville, the young soldier Mr Stockton used to be, whose face smiled up at her now from the wedding photograph, but for her own mixture of regret and happiness: regret because she knew that she would never see him again, and happiness in discovering that love was indeed, as she had always suspected, stronger than death.

HOW DOES YOUR GARDEN GROW?

Vivien Alcock

Old Mr Hewitt was ill. Again. An ambulance had carried him off to hospital. Again. In his garden, weeds began to grow among the flowers. Brambles sneaked under the fence and rioted behind the lavender. Roses dropped their petals untidily on the neat concrete paths. Everywhere plants spread out in the sunlight, like heedless children unaware of danger.

Mrs Hewitt came out through the french windows of her sitting room, and put a pair of gardening gloves on her fat red hands. She was a short, square woman, with a face like a painted brick.

Two pairs of eyes looked down at her from the apple tree on the other side of the fence; one pair frowning and intent, the other with a slitted yellow stare. The dark eyes belonged to Gina Hobb, a skinny girl with long black hair and a thin, pointed face. The yellow ones belonged to her grandmother's cat, Rumar, who was old and fat and lazy, his once black fur grown rusty from too much lying in the sun.

Mrs Hewitt was their enemy. They hated her.

The fat woman seemed unaware of the watchers in

the apple tree. Or perhaps she guessed they were there, knowing it to be their favourite perch, and was glad to have a helpless audience for what she was about to do. She put her hands on her hips and surveyed the unprotected garden with a nasty little smile. Then she walked towards the garden shed.

'Trip! Trip! Fall flat on your face!' Gina muttered, trying to will the woman's feet to stumble on the path. Mrs Hewitt disappeared into the shed.

The watchers glared at the closed door. Rumar, the cat, hated Mrs Hewitt because she threw stones at him whenever she saw him, and though she was a poor shot, she hit him occasionally, forcing him to scramble back over the fence in an undignified fashion, to the amusement of all the birds. He was too lazy, however, to be good at hating. Soon his eyes wandered away to watch the petals blowing over the paths, as if he was remembering the days when he'd been young enough to enjoy chasing such inedible toys.

But Gina was good at hating. She stared at the shed with her fierce black eyes, trying to will it to fall down on Mrs Hewitt's head.

'Crash, crush, crump,' she muttered.

Gina hated Mrs Hewitt for what she had done to the old man's garden. Every time Mr Hewitt had had to go into hospital, his wife had destroyed something he loved. First the trees went. Mrs Hewitt disliked trees because they were untidy and dropped their leaves where they chose, not respecting other people's property. Even the apple tree, on which Gina and Rumar sat, was lopsided. Over their garden, the branches grew to their full length, bowing down over a ragged lawn full of buttercups and dandelions. On the other side, the branches were chopped off short at the boundary fence. Not so much as a twig was allowed to grow over the garden next door.

'You're an old man now,' Mrs Hewitt had told her husband when he came home and saw what she had done. 'You don't want to spend your time sweeping up leaves.'

His grass had gone next, replaced by a square of concrete that would never need mowing.

'I have to look after you,' Mrs Hewitt had said, with her false smile. 'It's not good for you to be pushing that heavy mower at your age.'

And she had bustled back into her house, duster in hand, ready to pounce on any speck of dust that dared settle on her shining furniture, leaving Mr Hewitt standing in his treeless garden, looking sadly down at the square of concrete that had once been his treasured lawn.

'I'm sorry,' Gina had said from her perch in the apple tree. 'I couldn't stop her.'

He had smiled up at her. They were fond of each other, the gentle old man and the fierce young girl. They both liked living things; trees that shed leaves, flowers that dropped petals and harboured greenfly and welcomed bees, and cats that left their hair on furniture and sharpened their claws on table legs.

'She meant it kindly,' Mr Hewitt said, for he never complained. 'It's true I can't do as much as I used to. Oh well, perhaps it's all for the best.'

It made Gina angry that he was so meek. 'You should biff her one,' she advised. 'Stamp on her plastic flowers. Scratch her precious furniture. You can borrow Rumar for that, if you like. He's very good at it. Only wait till she's out or she'll throw things at him and he's too fat to run fast.'

Mr Hewitt had stopped her, shocked at these suggestions. 'I'm fond of my wife,' he'd said stiffly. 'Please don't say such things to me again, Gina.'

So now Gina said them to herself and her grandmother's cat and the leaves of the apple tree. She watched Mrs Hewitt come out of the garden shed, chopper in one hand, spade in the other, and muttered under her breath, 'What's she up to now, the horrible fat pig?'

The trees had gone. The grass had gone. Only the flowers were left. Surely she couldn't ... Even she wouldn't ... ?

Mrs Hewitt pulled up the flowers and left them with their roots drying out in the hot sun.

'What are you doing?' Gina shouted. 'They'll die if you leave them like that? What are you doing to his garden?'

Mrs Hewitt straightened up and looked with grim satisfaction at the furious face in the apple tree.

'Suppose you mind your own business and leave me to mine,' she said. 'My husband's ill in hospital. Someone has to see to things while he's away.'

'I'll do it! I'll look after his garden for him,' Gina promised anxiously. 'I'll do whatever you want me to – weed it, tie back the plants, sweep the paths. I promise. Please, Mrs Hewitt, please let me do it.'

In her agitation, she was bouncing up and down on her branch. A small leaf fell down into the garden next door. Mrs Hewitt picked it up between gloved finger and thumb, as if it were dirt, and tossed it back over the fence.

'If you've so much energy to spare, I suggest you do something about your own garden,' she said. 'It's a disgrace to the neighbourhood.'

Mrs Hewitt disliked Gina quite as much as the girl disliked her. She knew who posted dead leaves and old bus tickets through her letter-box. She knew who dropped sticky toffee papers onto her newly scrubbed front steps. She knew the hard green apple that had hit her on the head had not fallen from the tree next door, but had been thrown all too accurately by a small grubby hand. And so she had told the girl's grandmother who, to do her justice, had apologised handsomely and said that she would see that it did not happen again. Old Mrs Hobb was a lady and knew how to behave. How she'd ever come to have such a wild and wicked granddaughter was a puzzle.

With great pleasure, Mrs Hewitt told Gina what she was planning to do, knowing the girl was powerless to stop her.

'I'm going to have the whole garden covered with concrete,' she said, 'and them coloured paving stones laid on top. Orange and green I fancy – or maybe pink. There'll be plastic chairs that don't need taking in and out every time it rains, and a table with one of them striped umbrellas – like at the seaside. Everything nice and bright and neat, and no trouble to anyone. Now what have you to say to that, miss?'

'He'll hate it!' the girl cried, looking quite demented, with her black hair all tumbled and her black eyes blazing.

Mrs Hewitt turned her back on her and dug up a rose bush, chopping at its roots with her axe.

'You'll be sorry!' Gina screamed at her. 'I'll make you sorry for it!'

She jumped down from the apple tree and ran into the house to find her grandmother.

Mrs Hobb was in the kitchen, shelling peas. She was a thin, tall old lady, who must have been beautiful once, though her cheeks were now sunken and lined, leaving her nose too prominent on her narrow face. Her hair, though grey, was still thick, coiled at the back of her head and fastened with a silver pin. She was vain of her appearance. There were rings on her knobbly fingers, fine pearls hiding her scraggy neck, and her clothes were both expensive and fashionable.

She looked up when her granddaughter came banging in, and surveyed her with mild displeasure.

'What was all that vulgar screeching about?' she asked. 'Have you been quarrelling with Mrs Hewitt again? I thought I told you to leave her alone.'

'Gran, she's going to bury his garden in concrete! You've got to stop her! You've got to!'

Mrs Hobb held up her hand. 'There's no need to shout. I'm not deaf. Did you comb your hair this morning? It certainly doesn't look like it.'

Gina hastily smoothed her hair with her hands. 'He loves his garden, Gran. Don't let her destroy it. Please, Gran.'

Mrs Hobb's face softened, but she shook her head.

'I'm not going to interfere. I'm sorry, Gina, but after all, it's her garden. She can do what she likes with it, I suppose.'

'It's not hers! It's his! Can't you warn him –'

'No,' Mrs Hobb said firmly. 'It would be unkind – and quite useless. He's far too weak, in more ways than one. What she says goes in that house, like it or not.'

'I hate her! I hate her!' Gina raged, stamping on the floor in her fury.

'That's enough of that,' her grandmother said sharply. 'You're too fond of hating people, Gina. There's a wildness in you. I can't think where you get it from. I'm tired of apologising for your spiteful tricks. There's to be no more of them, do you understand?'

'Yes,' Gina muttered sulkily.

'No spiders in a chocolate box left on her doorstep. No molten wax poured down her outside lavatory. No slugs or snails tossed in through her open windows. You're to leave her alone, Gina, or you'll be in trouble.'

Three days later, workmen came with their machines into the garden next door and covered it with concrete, right up to the boundary fences on all sides. No longer would old Mr Hewitt smile with pleasure to see the first shoots poke up from the rich earth in spring. No longer would he talk to his flowers in summer. He would sit in a garden as neat and grim as a tomb, and wither away like his murdered flowers.

Gina could not sleep that night. She kept tossing and turning, seeing in her mind the concrete garden, as hard and grey as Mrs Hewitt's eyes.

I hate her, she thought, getting up and going over to the window. I hate her. I wish she were dead. Dead and buried in earth.

She stared down. The concrete garden was bleached by moonlight, a pale immaculate oblong, as cold as a tombstone.

I'd plant flowers on her grave, that would serve her right, Gina thought. No rest in peace for you when you're dead, Mrs Hewitt. Roots will nudge you in the dark, weeds wrap round your bones and squeeze and crack –

Crack! Like an echo of her thoughts the sound came, hard and sharp in the night air. Leaning out of her window, she saw the concrete was now marred by a jagged black line. She'd done it!

'Crack! Crack! Crack!' she commanded, and saw with delight dark lines spreading over the whole garden like a black spider's web.

She beat her fists on the windowsill with excitement and began to chant:

> 'Earth! Earth! Give up your dead.
> Every flower that died and bled,
> Ivy green and roses red,
> Bramble, thorn and poppy head,
> Rise! Rise! Rise!'

The cracks gaped wide, and out of each one came a writhing mass of tendrils, like thin grey snakes, bending their narrow heads to heave the broken concrete aside and make room for others to follow.

Gina leaned out of the window, her black hair blowing in the night wind, her eyes blazing. Then she turned and ran out of her room, down the stairs and out into the garden. The grass moved restlessly beneath her bare feet, and the air was filled with a strange scent, both sweet and rotten. She climbed the apple tree and looked down over the fence. The plants were thick and strong now, with pale leaves groping like hands and thorns as sharp as daggers.

'Revenge!' she shrieked. 'Kill! Kill! Kill!'

Mrs Hewitt had gone to sleep in front of her television set. She sat wedged upright in a small armchair, her hands folded in her lap, her ankles neatly crossed, and her mouth only slightly open.

A tidy sleeper in a tidy room. Everything was in its place. On the mantlepiece, the china shepherd and shepherdess were kept a proper distance apart, separated by a forbidding marble clock. Mr Hewitt's empty chair was immaculate, the cushions plump and undented, no messy newspapers scattered on the carpet beside it. The highly-polished furniture shone beneath the pink-shaded lights. The plastic flowers, newly washed that morning, made bright splashes of colour in their sparkling crystal vases.

Something tapped on the window.

Mrs Hewitt awoke with a start, smoothed her hair, pulled her skirt down over her fat knees, and looked round. The sight of her orderly room reassured her. Really, she thought, it's much easier to keep things nice without a man tramping in and out all the time. Not that she wouldn't be glad when Mr Hewitt came home, of course –

The tapping came again.

Who's that? she wondered, looking at the french windows.

She was a hard, selfish, mean-minded woman, but she did have a certain stubborn courage. Picking up a poker, she went over to the windows and peered out.

At first, she could only see her own face reflected, looking oddly pale and distorted. Then she noticed dim shapes moving behind the glass, long, thin and sinuous. Suddenly something flopped onto the window, and she stepped back, her heart thudding uncomfortably. It looked like a human hand, horribly misshapen. Then she realised it was a large leaf.

She went closer and pressed her nose against the glass, shading her eyes with her fingers. The window was covered with leaves. Twigs tapped insistently against the panes, like tiny drums calling an army to attack.

That girl! Mrs Hewitt thought furiously. This is one of her tricks. Piled up rubbish against my windows, has she? We'll see what her grandmother has to say about that.

Grunting, she undid the bolts and opened the doors wide. A swaying curtain of leaves and flowers hung before her, grey in the moonlight. Slashing her way through them with the poker, she strode out onto the terrace – stopped dead and stared.

Her whole garden was alive and crawling with plants. Giant brambles humped their way over the broken concrete like monstrous serpents. Ivy slithered and wriggled towards her feet. Huge roses turned their blind faces from side to side, as if trying to sniff out their prey.

They were coming for her, all of them! Something touched her ankle. Leaves gagged her mouth so that she could not scream. She tried to run back into the house, but they were behind her now: ivy and rose, bramble and poppy, lavender smelling of old ladies, lilies smelling of death. They pressed their soft, scented faces against hers, their thorns scratched her arms and tore at her hair. Brambles wound around her legs. Ivy crept up her arms. They were pulling her down, down, suffocating her, crushing her, wrapping her up in a shroud of flowers ready for her funeral ...

'No! No!' Gina cried in horror, appalled by what she had done. 'Gran! I didn't mean it! Gran!' she wailed, like a small child who had broken something precious.

Her grandmother was beside her, in a temper, black eyes burning hot enough to scorch. She climbed up the apple tree with surprising agility for one so old and frail-looking.

'Out of my way!' she cried, pushing so ferociously that the girl fell off her branch into the garden next door.

Her grandmother leapt down beside her and strode out over the mass of twisting, wriggling stems. She stopped some way from the house and held her arms up above her head; an odd-looking figure, tall and gaunt, her grey hair sticking out in two short plaits, and the sleeves of her cotton nightie falling back to show her skinny arms.

'Back! Back! Away with you!' she shrieked in a high, cracked voice. 'Back into your holes this minute, or I'll bring winter down on you! Frost that bites and kills! Snow that buries and breaks!'

With a sullen whisper of leaves and a crepitation of twigs, the plants slithered past her, baring their thorns like teeth, but not daring to touch her. Only the ivy defied her, coiling round her feet and hissing.

'Back, you impertinent weed!' she screamed in high fury, stamping on the ground so hard that it shook. 'Root-rot and leaf-blight infect you! Frog-fly and mealy-bug infest you! Lightning burn you! Secateurs snip you!'

The ivy fled after the others, back down through the cracks into the earth below. Now the garden was leafless again under the quiet moon.

Gina, crouching trembling on the ground, looked up nervously at her grandmother.

'That was clever of you, Gran,' she said, attempting an ingratiating smile.

But Mrs Hobb was not so easily appeased. She grabbed hold of her granddaughter's arm and dragged her towards the terrace.

'Come and see what you've done, you bad girl,' she said.

Mrs Hewitt lay flat on her back, her eyes shut, her

mouth open. Her face and arms were patterned with scratches, her hair ripped out of its tight curls, threads plucked from her dress, and her tights torn and laddered. Her breath whimpered painfully in her throat.

Mrs Hobb looked down at her. 'Well, at least she's still alive and not much hurt. That's a blessing. And more than you deserve – '

'I didn't mean it, Gran! I didn't, honestly. I didn't think it would work – it never has before. I – I sort of got carried away. But I didn't mean them to hurt her. Not really. Not like this.'

'Hmmm,' her grandmother said. 'Help me carry her in. Lord, what a weight ... Here, on the sofa. Put a cushion behind her head.' She stretched herself wearily, clutching her back, and scowled. 'Now I suppose I'll have to put things right again. It's too bad. I'm old and my bones ache, and I should be allowed to enjoy my retirement in peace. I'm fed up with you and your pranks, Gina,' she said, turning on her granddaughter, who shrank away nervously. 'I've a good mind ... ' Her eyes narrowed, and she began to trace patterns in the air with her thin, beringed fingers; slow, undulating patterns.

'No! No, Gran! Not a slug again!' Gina backed away, crying. 'Please! I'll be good! I'll never do it again. Please, Gran, not a slug. A toad, a wasp, anything – '

Her grandmother lowered her hands slowly. 'I'll give you one last chance, Gina. One more, that's all. Another trick like that, and I'll turn you into a slug – and forget the spell to bring you back. Your father wanted you brought up to a respectable profession. A doctor or a civil servant. He was right. You're far too wild to be a good witch. Now go and make some tea in her kitchen, and take your time about it.'

'What are you going to do, Gran?'

'Mind you own business, and do as I tell you.'

Gina went meekly into the kitchen, relieved at

having been let off so lightly. When she came back with the tea, she found her grandmother and Mrs Hewitt sitting side by side on the sofa like old friends. The scratches had vanished from Mrs Hewitt's face and her hair was back in its curls. Only her dress showed here and there a plucked thread that Mrs Hobb, growing shortsighted, had missed.

'I'd never have had that concrete laid if I'd known there was an underground stream beneath our gardens,' Mrs Hewitt was saying. 'It's hardly surprising it's cracked. I'll have to get it cleared away.'

'You want to put grass down,' Mrs Hobb said firmly. 'The roots hold the earth together. Grass and flowers and trees, that's what you need.'

Mrs Hewitt's face went pale, and she looked uneasily towards the window.

'Flowers,' she muttered. 'I suppose I do need flowers. I suppose, in the end, we all have to have them.'

THE CHARMER

Alison Prince

Nicky McBride sat on a rocky ledge at the foot of the cliff in the fading November daylight, her bag of schoolbooks wedged at her feet. The last lesson of the afternoon had been music – oh, and what music! The words of the song rang again in her mind as she gazed unseeingly at the wind-ruffled water. They might have been written specially for her.

Full fathom five thy father lies. Nicky sang the words aloud, though her voice was hardly audible out here against the noisy sluicing of the waves against the rocks.

> *Of his bones are coral made;*
> *Those are pearls that were his eyes;*
> *Nothing of him that doth fade*
> *But doth suffer a sea-change*
> *Into something rich and strange.*
> *Sea-nymphs hourly ring his knell;*
> *Hark! Now I hear them – Ding-dong, bell.*

Nicky sighed, leaning back against the cold rock. At school, the other girls had sung their way through the song with no particular interest, as if they were at hymn practice. But for Nicky, the words had jumped from the page. *Full fathom five, thy father lies.* In the stuffy music room, she had wanted to run out and come to this place which had been their own special haunt when he was alive. This was where those words belonged. Somewhere out in that water, her father had suffered a sea-change.

Lost, they called it. Lost at sea. It was a polite phrase, lacking the sodden heaviness of 'drowned'. But it was dreadfully appropriate, for his body had never been recovered. Nicky remembered again how he used to swing her up to ride on his shoulders if she got tired when they were out on their long walks. It seemed so high up, looking down on his curly dark hair.

It was getting colder. Nicky pushed her hands into the pockets of her school mac and hunched her shoulders. She would have to go home soon. Her mother didn't like it when she stayed late on the beach, though she had never said exactly why. But perhaps her father liked it. He was out there somewhere, a creature now of the wind and the spray and the salt sea. Up at the house, dry and brightly lit, he was just plain dead.

The wind brought a cold spatter of rain. Reluctantly, Nicky got up and slung her school bag over her shoulder. She climbed over the rocks until she reached the rough concrete steps which led up to the road, then went on up the steep wet pavement, past the small hotels and boarding houses, until she came to The Heights, absurdly turreted behind its fuchsia hedge. The Vacancies sign hung without real hope in the lounge window. There would be no visitors until the spring.

Nicky crossed the road to the house, dodging round a white sports car which was parked outside it, and climbed the steps leading to the back door. She went through the kitchen and into the hall to hang up her wet coat.

BEWARE! BEWARE!

There were voices upstairs. 'Mum?' called Nicky.

'Just a minute, dear!' Mrs McBride's voice held its professional cheerfulness, and Nicky's heart sank. Not visitors, surely? They were a pest which had to be put up with in the summer, like midges, but the winter should be free of them.

Nicky's mother came into the kitchen a few minutes later. Small and dark, her mass of curly hair and her quick movements gave her an air of constant energy. 'What a bit of luck!' she said. 'He wants a long-term let. Full board!'

Suddenly, Nicky couldn't answer. She felt robbed of the quiet winter by this stranger, but that was not all. The feeling which had swept over her was something much more powerful – a sense of terrible foreboding. With it came a new anguish of wanting her father to be here, strong and real. But he had been gone for five years, coral-boned under the sea. *Full fathom five.*

'What are you frowning about?' asked her mother.

'You always said you didn't want long-term residents,' said Nicky, trying to find an acceptable reason for her irrational antagonism. 'In case you fetched up running a home for geriatrics.'

Mrs McBride laughed. 'Oh, Mr Angelo isn't like that,' she said. 'He's quite young. Fortyish.'

'What's he doing here, then?' Nicky objected.

'He's an actor,' said her mother. 'Resting, he says, for the winter. Apparently he's got rheumatoid arthritis. Sad, really – but he's quite an amusing man. Really rather a charmer.'

Nicky tried to smile. 'That's nice,' she said. What was charm? A handsome face? Her father had been handsome. White pearls stared from a skull's eye-sockets, glimmering within the weed-grown bone. She shook her head irritably, trying to dispel the dread which filled her mind.

'You *are* in a funny mood,' her mother said, watching her.

'Yes,' Nicky admitted. 'Sorry.' Perhaps that's all it was – just a funny mood. *Ding-dong, bell.* 'I'll go and put my jeans on,' she said. Perhaps changing out of her school clothes might break the spell.

Nicky's room was at the front of the house, below the level of the steps which led up to the front door. Her mother slept at the back, in the small room next to the kitchen. The upstairs rooms were kept for visitors. Nicky hung up her navy blue school skirt and stepped into her jeans.

She was suddenly aware of a presence outside the rain-spattered window, and looked up in alarm. Then she smiled. A cat had jumped up onto the window sill. It uttered a yowling cry, its mouth suddenly wide in the dark, wet fur. Nicky pushed her feet into a pair of trainers and did up the laces. The cat yowled again, staring in with yellow eyes. She crossed the room and opened the window. 'What do you want?' she said, and ran her hand along the saturated fur. It felt as wet and slippery as seaweed.

The cat stepped in and rubbed its head against Nicky's hand in an ecstasy of gratitude. Without warning, it leapt onto her shoulder, purring loudly as it pushed its nose through her hair. Then it lay down, a cold, wet heaviness, and she could feel its purring vibrating through the back of her neck.

Nicky closed the window and went back to the kitchen with the cat on her shoulders. She said, 'Look what I've found. He was meeowing at the window.'

'Oh, *Nicky!*' said her mother. 'Do put him down, he's absolutely soaking wet. I wonder if he's been abandoned. Some of these summer-cottage people take on cats when they're here and then go off home and leave them.' She looked in the fridge and got out a left-over pilchard on a saucer. The cat leapt from Nicky's shoulder at the sight of it and yowled frantically.

'Can we keep him?' Nicky begged as the cat wolfed

down the pilchard. 'Please, Mum!' Mrs McBride had always contended that pets were an unnecessary expense.

'I don't know, Nicky, we'll have to see,' said her mother. 'I'll ask at Murchies' if anyone's lost a cat. I'll have to go down for some proper coffee – you can't really give Instant to a visitor.'

When her mother had gone out, Nicky gave the cat some milk, then took him back into her room. She had assumed that his coat was black, but now that it was drying, she could see that it was a dark, slaty grey, like the sky when a storm was blowing up. With complete self-possession, the cat jumped onto Nicky's bed and washed his face. Then he turned his head to stare at her with unblinking yellow eyes. Nicky sat down beside him. 'You shall stay,' she promised. They could perfectly well afford to keep a cat. Last summer, being for the first time old enough to help as a waitress, she had realised that The Heights was doing extremely well. But her sense of foreboding was as strong as ever.

Mr Angelo had his evening meal in the dining room, with the gas heater on to dispel the chill, while Nicky and her mother ate as usual in the kitchen.

'He says, will we join him for coffee,' Mrs McBride reported as she came back from taking the guest a slice of Black Forest Gateau from the freezer. 'I suppose it *is* a bit lonely in there, all by himself.'

Nicky frowned. She did not much like the dining room at the best of times, with its residual smells of gravy and the faint muskiness of many guests, but this evening there was something far more ominous about it.

'Oh, come on,' chided her mother, clattering cups onto a tray. 'Anyone would think the poor man was an ogre. Honestly, Nicky, he's –'

'Quite a charmer,' Nicky interrupted drily. 'Yes, I know. You said.' But she was ashamed of being so irrational. She made herself smile. 'Of course I'll come,' she said. 'Sorry. I'm a bit – tired or something.' She stood up helpfully and put some packs of sugar and cream on the tray. As she and her mother went towards the door, the cat, which had been asleep in front of the Aga, raised his head sharply, then ran across the floor and leapt onto Nicky's shoulder. His body felt tense, and he was not purring.

Holding the dining-room door open for her mother to go in with the tray, Nicky saw a ginger-haired man in a black velvet jacket getting up from the table by the window. 'This is a real pleasure,' he said. Then the smile froze on his face. He backed away. 'Would you mind,' he said. 'The cat – I'm allergic.'

'Oh, goodness,' said Mrs McBride. 'I'm so sorry. Nicky –'

But Nicky had already beaten a retreat to the kitchen. The cat's claws were gripping her shoulder. He leapt onto the kitchen table and turned, stiff-legged, to glare at the door. The fur on his back and tail had risen and he stood sideways to the invisible enemy, presenting an angry, defensive profile. Nicky stared at him, feeling the same prickle of horror down her own spine. 'But why?' she said to the cat. His yellow eyes glanced briefly into hers, then he shifted his gaze to the door as Nicky's mother came into the kitchen and said hurriedly, 'Darling, it's only the *cat* he's allergic to. Do come back, or it'll seem as if you're offended.'

Reluctantly, Nicky did as she was asked. This time, the actor's smile was well established. He wore an open-collared white shirt under the velvet jacket, with a zig-zag printed scarf tucked into it, and he limped a little as he stood up to pull a chair out for Nicky. 'I've got terrible feet,' he told her. 'Arthritis. Mucks me up in the winter. And to think I used to tap-dance.' He sketched a Fred Astaire gesture, and Nicky's mother looked sympathetic. 'What a shame,' she said.

'One of those things,' said Mr Angelo bravely. He

smiled at Nicky afresh. The line of his teeth was very straight and even. Not real ones, she thought. 'Awfully sorry about the cat,' he said. 'They just give me the shivers. Old Bill Shakespeare was right – Grey Malkin, the witch's familiar. A touch of the nasty about them. Shall I be mother?' He picked up the coffee pot without waiting for an answer, pouring a rapid stream into each cup with a waiter's aplomb. 'Let me guess,' he said teasingly to Nicky's mother, 'sugar no but cream yes. Am I right?'

She laughed. 'Quite right. Thank you, Mr Angelo.'

'Michael,' said the actor, and made a face. 'Always brings the house down,' he added, although neither Nicky nor her mother had laughed. 'Sugar for the beautiful daughter?' he asked, proffering the saucer of packets.

'No,' said Nicky. 'Thank you.'

'I suppose that's a stage name, is it?' Mrs McBride enquired. 'Michael Angelo.'

'Alas, no,' the actor confessed ruefully. 'My father was a juggler, Luigi Angelo. Worked with the family troupe, The Amazing Angeli. They used to do a marvellous act with chianti bottles – full ones. And my mother, God rest her soul, was an Irish theatrical landlady. Not being acquainted with the works of the Old Masters, she innocently called me after the blessed Saint Michael.' He sketched a sign of the cross. 'My father had returned to Verona and was unaware of my existence,' he added.

'Are you a Catholic?' asked Nicky's mother.

'Lapsed,' said Mr Angelo with a gusty sigh. 'My faith, my feet and most of my careers – all lapsed.'

Mrs McBride did not smile. 'I was going to say, there's a notice in the hall about church services, should you want to go to mass or anything,' she told him.

Mr Angelo smiled at her warmly. 'You know,' he said, 'you are a truly wonderful person. Full of strength and good sense.'

Nicky glanced sharply at her mother, and felt a surge of anger to see her smiling. Why didn't she find this flattery repulsive? Didn't she hear a warning bell? *Ding-dong, bell. Sea-nymphs hourly* –

As if taking up the theme, Mr Angelo said smoothly, 'Yes, your husband is a lucky man.'

Nicky felt her heart pounding in her chest.

The smile faded from Mrs McBride's face. 'My husband was lost at sea five years ago,' she said. 'He was in the Merchant Navy.'

Nicky watched the actor turn his head aside in a slow wince of sympathy, and horror mounted afresh in her mind. Why had he come here? 'I am so terribly sorry,' said Mr Angelo, his voice melting with sincerity. 'And you have run this place all on your own since then?'

'That's right,' said Nicky's mother. 'He always insisted that I had to be able to earn an income. It's as if he was – looking ahead. He bought this place on his last shore leave, and put in all the basic work on it.'

'And it's done well?' suggested Mr Angelo.

'Very well,' Mrs McBride admitted. 'The pension helped, of course, but – this sounds crazy, I know – I feel as if David still watches over it. He wouldn't let me make any wrong decisions.'

The actor shook his head in respectful amazement. 'Women like you make me feel humble,' he said.

Nicky almost gave a hysterical laugh. She clenched her hands under cover of the tablecloth, struggling to be sensible. The man was just a visitor, like any other. She forced herself to smile. 'These lapsed careers,' she said in the silence which had fallen. 'What were they?'

'Silver service waiter,' began Mr Angelo, ticking off the list on his fingers, 'electrician, bar tender, van driver, gardener, carpet dealer (and fitter), supplier of ersatz antique furniture – and griddle chef. To name but a few.'

'I can't see how you found any time for acting,' Nicky

heard herself remark. She blushed. She had not meant to give expression to this irrational loathing.

Mr Angelo looked hurt, and Nicky's mother said, 'That wasn't very kind, darling.'

'Oh, don't reprove her, Mrs McBride,' said the actor. 'The honesty of youth is good for us all.' He turned to Nicky, smiling again. His light brown eyes surveyed her carefully. 'What a charming name you have,' he said. 'Nicky – is it short for Nicola?'

'Veronica,' said Nicky.

'Ah!' Mr Angelo sat back, opening a hand to the air expansively. 'One of the most beautiful and dangerous passes in bull-fighting. And, of course, the purple-flowered shrub you have here in Scotland, proof against storms, friend of the salt spray. Grace and tenacity. Who could ask for more?'

Nicky stared into the light brown eyes. She tried to return his smile, but this time, her face would not work. Her stare, she knew, was full of antagonism. The actor's eyebrows rose slightly, and he turned away to Mrs McBride. 'And may I ask what *your* first name is?' he enquired.

'Jean,' said Nicky's mother.

'Jean McBride.' He sat back again, savouring it. 'Oh, yes. There's a Scottish comeliness about that which suits you. Though you are not Scottish yourself, are you?'

'I'm from Leicester.'

Say something romantic about *that*, the voice in Nicky's mind remarked – and again she met the actor's eyes. This time, he held her gaze with his own, coldly, until she was forced to look away. The defeat was devastating. Nicky felt her lips tremble as she drained her coffee cup, then she pushed her chair back from the table and ran out of the room.

The cat stood up, unhurried, as Nicky burst into the kitchen. He stretched, arching his back as if preparing for action, and pricked busily at the mat in front of the

Aga with his claws.

'Well, Grey Malkin,' said Nicky, trying to speak
lightly, 'What are we going to do, then?' She gathered
the cat into her arms and sat down by the kitchen table.
There had been no report from Murchies' of any missing
pet. Somehow, she had not expected that there would
be. She stroked and stroked Malkin's grey fur.

'What on earth's got into you?' asked Jean McBride
when she came back with the coffee tray some time
later. 'Was there any need for all that hostility?'

'I didn't mean to be hostile,' said Nicky with truth.
She couldn't explain what was happening to her, even
to herself. 'It's just – there's something creepy about
him.'

'Oh, don't be so silly,' said her mother. 'You made up
your mind before you ever saw the man that you weren't
going to like him. I can't have you being rude to the
guests, Nicky. And if we're going to keep that cat, you
must make sure he stays in the kitchen.'

It was all too much. Nicky jumped to her feet, clutching the cat in her arms. 'Why don't you lock us both
up?' she heard herself shout. 'Then you'd be happy,
wouldn't you?' And she fled with Malkin to the safety
of her bedroom.

Several weeks dragged by. Nicky went to school as
usual, but she sat in a dream as she thought of Mr
Angelo spreading his charm through the house like the
sticky syrup in a fly-catching plant. The days shortened
and the weather was wet and windy, but she still picked
her way across the rocks after school to sit for a while
and stare out across the sea. At these times the nightmare would fade a little and, leaning back against the
rock with the sea spray kissing her closed eyes, she
would know that there would be an end to all this
horror. Reassured, she would start back to the house,
but as she climbed the steep cliff road, the presence

of Mr Angelo would spread out to meet her, and her confidence disintegrated like the sea water which broke so boldly across the rocks and then, in a hundred insignificant trickles, seeped away.

Nicky's mother seemed happy, humming to herself as she bustled round the kitchen in her plastic apron with a picture of a bottle of tomato sauce on it. But Malkin brooded and skulked, sneaking through the door whenever he could, to present himself before Mr Angelo.

'Nicky, this cat really will have to go if you can't keep him out of Mike's way,' said Jean McBride one Saturday morning as she shoed Malkin ahead of her into the kitchen. 'That's three times this morning I've had to move him. He was outside the bathroom door, then in the dining room, and just now Mike couldn't get into the lounge because of him. And it's not funny!' she added fiercely as Nicky failed to repress a smile.

'No,' Nicky agreed. Her mother was right. It was not funny. It was an exhausting struggle which she would like to give up. But whether she wanted it or not, she was locked in a dreadful battle with Mr Angelo. And her mother was the prize.

'Don't look at me like that,' said Jean. 'And for goodness sake, Nicky, do stop this absurd vendetta against Mike. Apart from anything else, having him here is nice extra money at this time of year.'

'I'll give up piano lessons,' Nicky heard herself say. 'I won't go to a disco again, ever.'

'That's just ridiculous,' snapped her mother.

Nicky got up and fetched her mac from the hall, fielding Malkin as he attempted to slip through the door again.

'You can't go out in this,' Jean protested. 'It's pouring with rain.'

'I don't care,' said Nicky, pushing her feet into her wellingtons. She had to go down to the rocks. It would be better out there.

'Well, I think you're being utterly childish. Just for once we get a visitor who's amusing to talk to, and you throw a stupid little fit of jealousy.'

Nicky turned to face her mother. 'All right,' she said with a calmness which was not of her making. 'Believe that if you want to. But you're the one who's being stupid. Be careful,' her voice said. 'Be very careful.' Appalled by her own cheek, Nicky bent down to pick up the cat, then bolted out of the kitchen and down the steps to the road. She crossed over in the heavy rain and paused beside the railings at the cliff's edge. Far below, the full tide crashed against the rocks, and Nicky could taste the salt spray on her lips, mingled with the rainwater which already ran down her face.

Malkin began to struggle in her arms, and when Nicky let him go, he ran back across the road and up the steps to the house. Nicky pushed her hands into her mac pockets and began to walk down the hill to the beach.

Rain hissed across the sand. Water found its way in through Nicky's mac and spread with cold intimacy across her shoulders, reminding her of Malkin's cold wet heaviness when he had first arrived, on the same day as Mr Angelo.

After a while, Nicky was so saturated that she began to enjoy it. Water trickled down her spine and her feet swam in her wellington boots, but she was warm inside her sodden clothes as she walked fast along the sand to the pier and then back to the rocks. By the time she reached the ledge where she so often sat, her fingers were tingling and she felt full of energy. 'I belong out here,' she said aloud, and laughed as she shook a shower of drops from her hair. Everything was going to be all right.

As if in confirmation, the clouds parted and a faint yellow sun gleamed through the rain which still roughened the water further out across the bay. A rainbow's transparent arc stood in the sky like a bridge between cloud and horizon. *Nothing of him that doth fade*, Nicky thought, *But doth suffer a sea-change Into something rich and strange*.

She gave a little shiver. She was too wet to sit still for long. Jumping from rock to rock, she made her way down to the sea's edge and waded along in the shallow water. Once past the weed-dripping pillars of the pier, the sand gave way to shingle, but Nicky walked on. The rainbow faded and fresh banks of cloud piled up. Heavy drops of rain began to fall again, and Nicky's optimism left her. She could not walk about in the rain all day. She turned away from the sea and went up the shelving beach to the road.

Halfway up the hill, a white sports car screeched to a halt beside her. Nicky felt her scalp prickle. There was no need to look round. She knew who it was. She could hear the car's windscreen wipers swishing busily.

'Nicky!' Mr Angelo shouted after her from the car's window. 'Wait!' Nicky walked on, but the car caught up with her again, and he leaned across and opened the door. 'Don't be daft,' he said. 'Get in. Your mother's worried sick about you.'

Nicky stared at him, unable to pull her eyes away. She saw the ridges in the forehead above the light brown eyes, saw the reddish skin on his nose, the corrugated ginger hair. The freckled hand patted the seat beside him invitingly. 'Come on,' he said. 'Don't be stupid.'

'I like walking,' Nicky muttered.

Mr Angelo laughed, but the charm had been stretched too thin, and now it gave way. 'You like walking and you don't like me,' he said. 'That it?'

Nicky felt hot colour flood her cheeks. Grown-ups were not supposed to say such naked, school-yard things.

'Can't quite bring yourself to say it, can you?' sneered Mr Angelo. '*Such* a nicely-brought-up girl. But I'm telling you, darling, you're making the mistake of your life. I could be the best friend you and your mother ever had.'

'What do you mean?' asked Nicky unwillingly. She wanted to back away from the car until she felt the railings at the cliff's edge behind her, then she would be able to turn and run. As it was, she found herself obliged to go on holding open the car's door in the rain while Mr Angelo leaned his elbow across the back of the passenger seat and stared up at her.

The thin lips twisted in a smile. 'So you want confidences, do you?' he mocked her. 'All the ins and outs of what my plans are. You've got to be joking, darling. Stuff like that is for my friends.' It was a shock to hear how different he sounded out here. Gone were the cultured voice and the graceful gestures. 'I am a very friendly person,' he added with menace. 'You'll learn that in time. Or you won't.' He reached for the door, then thought of something else. 'And about that cat,' he added. 'If you keep putting it in my way, it'll have a nasty accident.'

Standing motionless in the rain with her hand on the car door, Nicky began to tremble. She felt very cold, but she could not move.

'It was out on the road this morning,' the man went on. 'And a cat is no match for a car. Don't say I didn't warn you – *darling*.' He slammed the door shut, snatching it from Nicky's numb fingers, and drove away with a contemptuous squeal of tyres.

'Darling, *do* cheer up,' said Jean McBride as she put a butterfly of lemon on Mr Angelo's grilled sole that evening. 'I just don't know what's got into you.'

Nicky sat morosely by the Aga with the cat clasped in her arms. 'He said he was going to run over Malkin,' she said. It was different now. It was open warfare.

Jean looked up, startled.

' "A cat is no match for a car",' Nicky quoted. 'That's what he said.'

'You must have misunderstood,' said her mother, wiping her fingers briskly.

'That's what I *thought* you'd say,' retorted Nicky. A tear ran down her nose and she scrubbed it away angrily with her sleeve, ducking her head.

Her mother came and stooped down in front of her, taking Nicky's hands in hers across the purring bulk of Malkin and giving them a little shake. 'Listen,' she said, 'I'm sure he wouldn't do anything so dreadful. He speaks about you with such affection and understanding. I'm *sure*, Nicky.'

Tear-glazed, Nicky looked at her. 'What would you do if he did?' she asked.

'I'd tell him to go,' said her mother promptly. 'That's how sure I am, you see? I can promise I'd tell Mike to go, because I know I'd never have to.'

Nicky nodded slowly, and said no more.

When her mother had gone into the dining room with Mr Angelo's tray, the tears which Nicky had tried to suppress overwhelmed her, dropping in great blobs on Malkin's grey fur. She stroked them away gently. He was such a hard sacrifice to make – but the way was clear now. It was the only chance. The cat's yellow eyes stared up at her steadily. 'You know, don't you?' Nicky whispered, and felt a shiver run down her back. 'That's what you came to do. You were sent here to get rid of Mr Angelo. Oh, Malkin – whose familiar are you?'

That night Nicky woke with a start, listening intently for a repeat of the sound which had broken into her dream. What had it been? A footfall? A stifled laugh? Malkin jumped off the bed and she saw him by the orange light of the street lamp which shone through her curtains, standing with his nose pressed to the crack of the door. 'What is it?' Nicky breathed.

The house was silent. Gradually Nicky relaxed again. She pulled the duvet up over her shoulders and turned on her side – but the cat began to scratch urgently at the door, hooking his claws underneath it to rake noisily at the wood.

'Do you want to go out?' Nicky asked, sleep-fuddled. She got up and opened the window, then picked Malkin up and carried him across to it, but the cat struggled free and ran back to the door, where he began an even more frantic assault on it. 'Malkin, don't,' said Nicky. 'You'll wreck the paint, and Mum will be furious.' She took the cat back to bed with her and stroked him soothingly, hoping he would settle down, but his tail swished angrily, and the minute she let him go, he ran back to attack the door again.

Nicky's scalp prickled. Was he trying to escape from the fate she had planned for him? She lay back on her pillows and put her hands over her face, overwhelmed with guilt and misery. It was silly to think he was a supernatural being. He was just a cat. Like a re-run film, she saw herself standing by the railings with Malkin in her arms as the white sports car approached. It was not her fault, she would say afterwards. She had tried to prevent him from jumping into the road. Mr Angelo had driven over him on purpose.

No. She couldn't do it.

The clawing went on, and Nicky got out of bed and put her dressing gown on. 'I'll give you some milk,' she said to the cat in apology for the unspeakable deed she had planned. He stared up at her, waiting. But the minute she opened the door he was out of it, disappearing like a grey streak into the darkness of the basement hall.

Nicky padded into the kitchen and poured some milk into a saucer. 'Malkin!' she called in a whisper. 'Where are you?' She went into the hall and began to grope her way across it. The door of her mother's room stood ajar. Had Malkin gone in there? Nicky stood irresolutely, not daring to switch the light on for fear of waking her mother. Tomorrow was Sunday, she reasoned. Guests had their breakfast late on Sundays. There would be plenty of time for Nicky to retrieve Malkin in the morning, before the dreadful man came out of his room upstairs.

Nicky went back to her own room, and to be on the safe side set her alarm clock for half past seven. Then with her door propped open so that Malkin could return if he chose to, she went to sleep.

It was still dark when Nicky was shocked into consciousness for a second time by a complex thunder of bumps, followed by a gasping sob. She leapt out of bed and ran into the hall, this time not hesitating to switch on the light. Her mother lay huddled in her dressing gown at the foot of the stairs, both hands clasped round her ankle. Nicky knelt beside her. 'Mum!' she said. 'What happened?'

'I slipped,' said Jean, her face contorted with pain. 'Malkin was lying on the stairs. I didn't see him in the dark. That cat, Nicky, honestly –' She bit her lip, unable to say more.

'It'll have to go,' said Mr Angelo from the top of the stairs. 'Jean, are you all right?' He came down towards them and Nicky backed away. His pale, freckled legs were bare under his dressing gown.

'Your mother brought me a hot drink because I couldn't sleep,' Mr Angelo explained righteously. 'And this is what happens.' He knelt down beside Jean and put his hand on the injured ankle, confident, Nicky noticed, that she would not object. 'Can you wriggle your toes?' he asked her. Jean shook her head, and tears swam in her eyes. 'I think you've broken it,' the actor said. 'Let's get you somewhere more comfortable, then I'll ring your doctor. Nicky, put the light on in your mother's room, please.'

Nicky did as she was asked. It was hard to believe that this smooth, well-modulated voice belonged to the man who had spoken so roughly to her yesterday. She watched with a mounting sense of unreality as the

actor stooped and picked up Jean McBride as if she had
been a child, carrying her into the bedroom to lay her
on the unrumpled bed. There was no sign of his usual
limp.

'Amazing what you can do if you've got to,' he said,
aware of Nicky's eyes on him.

'Use the telephone in the kitchen, Mike,' said Jean.
'The one in the hall is just a coin-op for the visitors.'

Mr Angelo, limping again, went off to invade their
private quarters. Nicky met her mother's eye, then
looked away. So the actor was not a visitor. He had
become something else.

Dawn was breaking as the white sports car drove off
to the hospital, preceded by the doctor's Rover. Jean
McBride did not wave from her seat beside Mr Angelo.
Shivering, Nicky closed the front door and crept back
to bed. Malkin, who had been notably absent while Mr
Angelo made everyone a cup of tea, was curled up in
the middle of the duvet, comfortably asleep.

'Why did you do that?' Nicky shouted at him, shaking
the cat by the scruff of his neck to wake him from his
uncaring slumber. 'It's my *mother* you've hurt! And now
that man is going to take over the whole house, don't
you see?' Then she clutched Malkin closely in an agony
of regret. It was too late for recriminations. Her mother
had agreed with Mr Angelo that the cat must go. And
how could Nicky object? She had herself planned to
use Malkin's life for her own purpose. But now everything had changed.

Nicky lay awake as the grey light strengthened, her
brain churning amid cobwebs of horror. She could see
ahead with appalling clarity. Mr Angelo, with his many
claimed abilities, would take over the running of the
house while Nicky's mother was laid up. And when
the broken ankle was better, what then? Would Jean
blushingly announce that Mike was to be Nicky's new
father? The actor had already made a head-of-the-

household statement about Malkin, dismissing Jean's suggestion that they should try to find the cat an alternative home. 'I think not,' he had said. 'This habit of hiding on the stairs really is pretty dangerous. I should feel terribly responsible if the cat caused somebody's death.'

Nicky turned her head from side to side on her pillow. Tomorrow would be Monday, and as soon as she was safely out of the way at school, Mr Angelo would ring up the vet. This coming day was to be Malkin's last. Nicky sat up and stared at the sleeping cat. He looked small and ordinary now, defenceless against the needle which would slide death into his veins. The idea that he had a sense of purpose was a fragile defence which Mr Angelo had destroyed. Nicky gathered the cat into her arms and wept.

'Darling, they don't suffer,' said Jean, sitting in the kitchen with her plastered leg resting on a footstool. 'It's just like an anaesthetic, only they don't wake up.'

'You can have a dog,' said Mr Angelo briskly, stirring the teapot then rinsing the spoon under the tap. 'Nice little Jack Russell. Just the job.'

It was starting already, Nicky thought. He sounded grotesquely fatherly. Never. Oh, never. *Full fathom five thy father lies.* 'I don't like dogs,' she said, although she would have jumped at the chance once. In that other life, before all this had started.

He shrugged, turning to Jean in smiling appeal. 'I do try,' he said. 'Never mind. What d'you fancy for lunch? Salade niçoise, perhaps, and omelettes?'

'How lovely,' said Jean. 'Nicky knows where everything is – I'm sure she'll help you.'

'No need,' said Mr Angelo quickly. 'I've worked in enough hotel kitchens to cope with a little thing like lunch for three. Have you got the Sunday papers?'

''Murchies' don't deliver on a Sunday,' Jean explained. 'Nicky usually pops down for them.'

THE CHARMER

The actor gave a dismissive sweep of his hand. 'Why
walk when there's a car outside?' he said. 'I'll just pour
you a cup of tea, then I'll run down to the shop. Then
you ladies can spend a nice relaxing morning reading
all the scandal while I cook you a gourmet lunch.'

His eyes met Nicky's, cool and mocking. He's busy
being the best friend we ever had, she thought bitterly.
Whether I like it or not. I've lost. It's all over.

'Nicky,' her mother began when Mr Angelo had gone
out, 'you really will have to accept that Mike will be
running things for a while.'

Nicky said nothing.

Jean leaned her head back against her chair. 'Oh,
Nicky,' she said helplessly, 'don't spoil it. I didn't know
how lonely I've been. Not until Mike came.'

Nicky's thoughts were splintering into fragments of
love and fury. She shut her eyes, trying to find some
way to express the turmoil, but there was only a desire
to be out of this house and away from the useless fight.

'Can I let the cat out for a little while?' she heard
herself ask. 'While – Mike – is getting the papers?'

'Yes, of course,' Jean said wretchedly. 'I really am
sorry about Malkin, Nicky.'

'Yes.' Nicky's voice was dispassionate as she echoed
her mother's words. 'Of course.'

Malkin, who had been imprisoned in Nicky's room,
jumped through the window when she opened it,
running up the steep bank of the garden to disappear
under the shrubs. Nicky decided that she had better
keep an eye on him. There was no point now in making
things any worse. She climbed over the window sill
after him, into the garden.

The cat emerged from under a bush and looked at
her, tail high as if in invitation. Then he ran down the
steps to the road's edge.

'Malkin, be careful!' called Nicky. A cat is no match

for a car. And in the instant of remembering those words, she knew what Malkin meant to do. Rather than wait for the vet's needle tomorrow, he would end his life in his own way, under the wheels of Mr Angelo's returning car. His sense of purpose was not, after all, of Nicky's imagining. And this was his last chance.

Nicky was appalled. 'Malkin, no!' she cried. 'It's too late!' Her mother would never tell the wonderful Mike to go now, whatever happened. 'Malkin, come here! Don't, it's for nothing!'

The cat turned his head and looked at her, then deliberately ran across the empty road and down the hill a little way. Nicky followed him frantically. A light, misty rain had begun to fall. Far below, the full tide lapped gently against the rocks. Nicky paused in her pursuit of the cat and stared out, almost unwillingly, across the sea. Gradually her racing pulses calmed. So this was the end, she thought. The battle was lost, but at least it was over. 'Malkin,' she said reasonably, 'do come here. Please.' There was no need to see the mangled body, the blood on the wet road.

The cat crouched in the coarse grass which grew on the cliff top, and Nicky knelt down and reached for him between the railings. She managed to grab him by the scruff of his neck and hauled him, unresisting, towards her. Then she stood up, holding the cat firmly, her back to the road. She could hear the car coming up the hill, but she did not turn to look at it. She gazed instead at the perfect line of the horizon, where the colourless water met the gently-weeping sky. It would always be there, she thought. Nothing else mattered.

The car's engine was loud in her ears. She turned to let the vehicle go past, leaning back against the railings. And in that instant, the cat gave a convulsive leap and sprang out of her arms, straight into the path of the fast-moving car. Brakes screamed. The white sports car slewed across the road, jumped the far kerb and bounced off the garden wall of the Sea View Hotel.

Malkin, untouched, leapt into the garden of The
Heights which adjoined it and watched with arched
back as the car somersaulted across the road.

To Nicky, frozen with horror, the car seemed to come
towards her with astonishing slowness. Its doors burst
open like the wings of a great white bird. The strength
of the railings against which she leaned was suddenly
gone, and as she fell out into emptiness, the sky wheeled
around her and the horizon swung vertically across her
vision as the song which had haunted her in these last,
long weeks rang finally in her mind. *Ding-dong, bell.
Ding-dong –*

'Mrs McBride,' began the policeman carefully, 'it seems
that there is one small crumb of comfort to be gleaned
from this tragedy. Dental records confirm that the man
calling himself Michael Angelo was, in fact, a confidence trickster called John Albert Leeson. You yourself have almost certainly had a lucky escape. This
man has been associated with a number of unexplained
deaths, always of widowed ladies like yourself, and
always in circumstances where he has benefited from
the resulting estate, but until now we've never –'

The policeman paused and glanced uneasily at the
Home Help who had let him in. She shrugged. Jean
McBride, sitting with her plastered foot resting on a
stool in front of the Aga, showed no sign of having
heard what had been said. She stared unblinkingly into
the eyes of the grey cat which lay purring on her lap.

'Mrs McBride?' the policeman prompted gently. 'Did
you hear me?' Receiving no answer, he added, 'I am so
very sorry about your daughter's death. It must have
been a terrible shock.' But it was not until the cat
reached out a long paw to touch the woman's face as if
reproving her that she looked up, and then her eyes
seemed to be gazing at some far horizon. 'Nicky's all
right,' she said. 'She and her father have always been
very close. We'll be all right now.'

BEWARE! BEWARE!

The policeman glanced at the Home Help again in consternation, and she made a face then shook her head. Jean McBride did not seem to see either of them. Her gaze had returned to the cat's yellow eyes, and she smiled as she stroked and stroked the grey fur.

NIGHTMARE

Berlie Doherty

Rab lives over the railway lines, near the allotments. He doesn't always live there; sometimes I don't see him for weeks or even months, and then he just turns up again as if he's never been away. He lives in an old shed that needs pulling down – it's more of a barn really, with high heavy doors. He says it's all that's left of his estate, that long ago his family lived in a big house that was bombed in the war, and that all the allotments are really on his land. His granddad's a horse-dealer; they go round the country together to horse fairs and markets. I don't think Rab gets to school much; he's supposed to go to the one by the allotments when they're here, but I don't think he's got a lot of time for that sort of learning. They're a bit like gypsies, really. I'm not supposed to have anything to do with him, but I do. I can't help it. If you knew Rab you'd understand.

He hangs round and waits for me to come over the hill from school, and I see him leaning against the big chestnut tree or sitting astride the wall near our house and I think 'Great! Rab's back!'

I wish he hadn't come this winter though.

'Coming on moors?' he asks me, as if I only saw him yesterday. 'Coming up to Downpour?' And before I know it I've run in to change into old clothes that I'm allowed to get mucky, and I'm racing over the moors with him, scrambling over those massive boulders that he says are fossilised dinosaur droppings, and slithering behind the waterfall to the dark cave behind it that we call the Downpour Den. 'Cavemen lived here,' he tells me, and his voice bounces round the dripping hollows. 'You're standing on the dust of their bones.' I know it's true. 'We'd be all right here, if there was a Big Bang. We could come here and live.'

Rab isn't a house person. He isn't much older than me, but he knows everything. I'm sure that's because he isn't a house person. He lives in the hut with his granddad, Ged, who's a grimy-looking cold and sour fellow; he never speaks to me; I'm not sure I like him at all. And when they feel like going they just go. I hate it. I never know they've gone. I go down to their hut and try to peer in through the one high window, but they have stringy curtains draped across and there's nothing to see in there. There's a smell of Rab and Ged though, whether they're there or not. People have tried to get that hut knocked down while they're away, but they can't. It belongs to Rab and his granddad. It's their home.

'I wish you wouldn't go without telling me,' I say to him. 'I hate that, not saying goodbye and that.'

That always makes him laugh. 'What's the point of saying goodbye?' he says. 'I know I'll be coming back.'

Last time Rab turned up was in the dead of last winter. I wish I hadn't seen him. It was after Christmas, and I was just going up our road to the post and there he was, hunched up in the cold by the chestnut tree. The snow had come a few days before and now it was packed ice.

It was an effort to walk upright.

'All right, Rab?' I shouted, pleased to see him, but not showing it.

'Coming up to Downpour?' he asked me.

'Eh, it's freezing!' I said. 'We'll never get over moors in this lot.'

'Get your boots on,' he told me, not even looking at me, holding his white hands up to his mouth as though he was trying to melt his fingers with his breath. 'See you at moorgates. There's something I want to tell you.'

I always do what Rab says. I can't help it. Half an hour later I'd got my thickest clothes on and my boots and I was standing by the white stile that leads off up to the open moorland, stamping on a patch of ice that was iron-hard. Nothing moved. The sun was lemon-yellow but there was no heat from it at all, and all the blades of grass and bells of dead heather were clamped in their own ice-shells.

I heard Rab whistle, and I saw him come out onto the footpath about a quarter of a mile on from where I was standing. I waved and swung myself over the stile, lost my footing on the last slippery step and sprawled head first into the ice-blades. By the time I'd picked myself up Rab was out of sight, but I knew the way off by heart and slithered after him, my heart jerking into my throat every time I lost my footing. I caught up with him at the Edge. He was sitting with his legs dangling over a drop of nearly a hundred foot, looking out across the deep white floor of the valley. I eased myself onto the slab next to him. In summer you can hear the curlews up here, and the cackling of the grouse on the moors, and the sheep yelling to each other across the slopes, but today, when my panting had died down, there was nothing. Not a sound.

'Everything's died,' I said.

'The winter solstice,' Rab said. 'Everything's standing still. The sun, and the grass, and the streams, and the birds. Nothing moving.'

'You'd think it was waiting for something.'

'There's nothing to wait for now. It's too late.'

You don't expect Rab to sound like that, with that kind of sadness in his voice. He pulled himself up and spat over the Edge. We listened out for the tiny splat as it struck rock, and laughed. That was more like it.

'Gozzing's good for you,' he told me. 'Clears your passages. If you swallow your gozz it clogs up all your works.'

He set off carefully over a boulder that was completely cased in ice, and then started running, his boots striking the iron of the ground like flints, a kind of urgency; I lost sight of him as he ran and could only hear the chime of his stride, and then I heard nothing but my own steps as I stumbled and slid, and the rapid rasp of my breath. I skidded at last down the slope to the Downpour, and brought myself to a halt against the squat stone we called toad-rock. From here the narrow track twists round and comes below the cascading force of the waterfall. Because of the twist of the valley you don't hear anything from this side of toad-rock. As soon as you scramble round it to the jut of the path you're deafened by its clamour; it drowns out everything, and the spray from it showers over you – no escaping till you ease yourself behind it into the den.

I edged myself round the glassy rock-foot, and then I was struck by the weight of silence. The whole waterfall was frozen – I could see great limbs of icicles sprouting from the overhang, and the green-white sheen of a huge slab of ice draped across the mouth of Downpour Den, like a curtain. The silence was heavier than the noise I'd expected – it was like a pressure waiting to burst, waiting to explode into splinters and tumble down the boulder scree to the valley.

Rab was clinging onto a rock near the overhang, and I made my way over to him, hugging the slippery skin of the stones with both hands as I went; but when I reached him and looked up at last into the frozen

curtain that hung over the Downpour I saw something
that was so terrifying that I'll never get it out of my
mind, that I think of every day, as if it's part of me now.
It was this: a horse, trapped in the ice; a great black
horse, its legs straddled so its hooves were planted
firmly in bed-rock, its head lifted, teeth bared in fright,
its eyes staring; locked in death.

I think I crawled back up on my hands and knees till
I was on ground where I felt safe enough to stand, and
then I started running, feet splaying out each side of
me, my head pounding and dizzy; when I couldn't
breathe any more I turned round to wait for Rab, but
he was nowhere in sight. I could have sworn I'd heard
him scrabbling back up the slope after me, and the thud
of his boots on the hard rocks. I waited a bit but the
cold began to seep into me; I couldn't stop myself from
shaking, still in shock from the sight of the horse frozen
into its glassy tomb. Besides, Rab knew many routes
over the moors – he could be anywhere. I jogged back
home, glad of the comforting warmth of our house, and
the quiet normal talking of my mum and dad in the
kitchen.

I couldn't sleep that night. Mum had gone to bed
early and Dad was playing his jazz in the front room.
Usually I love to listen to music when I'm in bed; in the
end it always drowses me off to sleep. I went downstairs
and got myself a drink, then wandered into the back
room. We don't use that room much in winter; it's a
cold room, because we're on the edge of town and the
wind comes off the moors onto the back of the house,
and we made the mistake of putting big sliding door-
windows in to give us a better view. I went over to the
window now. The curtain had been pulled across to
keep out the draught, but I thought I'd like to look at
the moors in the moonlight, the blue-white gleam of the
snow. Just before I reached the window I heard Rab's
voice, calling my name very softly from outside. It was
almost as if I'd known he'd be there.

BEWARE! BEWARE!

I tugged at the curtain with one hand, sipping at my hot chocolate, and there instead of the sliding window was a huge slab of ice, and frozen into it, the black horse.

Its eyes were wide open and its ears pressed back, and its yellow teeth were bared in fright. As I watched in the same lock of fear it reared back its head. In slow motion its front legs carved an upwards arc and flung black hooves to pound against the ice; I could hear the sweet breathy sound of the saxophone in the other room, and I could hear the pounding of the hooves, and the ice tearing in front of me, above and around me, the splintering and crinkling as a thousand tiny bright shards showered over me, sharp as glass, bright as water. Hooves flailed as the black horse reared again, with hot life snorting from his nostrils. And clinging on to his back, laughing down at me, was Rab.

'Come on!' he shouted. 'Up on moors.' He leaned down, one arm tucked into the horse's mane, and heaved me up in front of him.

I can feel the way my legs ached as they stretched across the black sinewy back, and the lurching sensation beneath me as we galloped over the moors. I'd never ridden a horse in my life, and I was jolted from side to side and up and down with the unfamiliar movement. Rab had his arm round my waist to stop me from slipping off, and I remember the ice-cold pressure of his fingers. I dug my fingers into the mane and clung onto it; it felt like thick, silky hair. The air on my cheeks was raw, and as we plunged into the black bitter night, away from the houses, away from the lights, I felt as if all my known world was slipping away from me; and that this was where I'd rather be, riding forever in cold air. We soared over the white stile of moorgates and thundered up the familiar whitened tracks, with the stars hanging and turning like icicles. Gleaming boulders loomed up and away from us. We were streaming fast, floating; we were in a different element, like water.

I recognised the squat bulk of the toad-stone, where the scree slope fell away from us; I recognised the splintered ice-curtain of the Downpour, and as the horse leapt across the mouth of it into the black cavern behind I tried to slide off his back ...

'No!' I screamed. 'Not there!'

Rab laughed, his ice-cold hands pressing into my ribs, and his laugh echoed and bounced in the hollows of the caves. 'Stay with me,' he urged. 'Don't leave me.'

I heard a creaking above my head, and watched the slow languorous curtain of ice slide down to envelop the cave, felt the intense chill of it as it scraped across my skin, trapping me ...

My dad found me standing in the dark in the back room. He took the cup of cold chocolate out of my hand.

'You've had a nightmare,' he said. 'You're all right.'

I jerked back the curtain, expecting to find the window shattered, and the snow on the lawn outside swirled round with the kicking of hooves, but there was nothing to see, only the moors cold and quiet in the moonlight, and the stars, like twisting icicles.

'There was a horse,' I told Dad. 'It carried me off to the Downpour ...'

He lead me back upstairs to my room. 'People used to think,' he told me, 'that wild horses came in the night and carried them off to terrible places. That's why it's called a nightmare. Go to sleep now. You'll be all right.'

But I had no intentions of sleeping ever again. I sat bolt upright in my bed with the light on, listening out for the stamp of hooves on the iron earth, and for Rab. Laughing.

The next day was the beginning of the new term. It stayed just below freezing all day, but the sun was bright and the sky was a kind of fierce blue. It was the sort of day that Rab and I liked to go up on the moors, when you could see for miles from the Edge, all the little villages and roads in the valley, and the river winding slowly through. I couldn't get Rab off my mind that day. I wanted to tell him about my dream. I wondered if he'd had the same one. We'd tried to do that many times – we'd told each other that we would try to dream the same thing, and meet up in our dreams. We'd nearly done it once – we'd both dreamt of the Downpour Den one night, but there'd been no people in either of our dreams. Why had he laughed, in my dream? Why had he wanted to be trapped in the ice-cave, when I'd been so frightened? And even as I thought of all these things that I wanted to ask him about, the idea came to me just as powerfully as it had done last night, that it hadn't been a dream at all, but that it had really happened.

And there was another thing that bothered me. When we'd gone up to the Downpour yesterday he'd said there was something he wanted to tell me. He'd taken me to see the horse, but he hadn't told me anything, except that it was the winter solstice. I knew that. I knew that we'd had midwinter's night before Christmas, and that it was as if nothing grew around that time, waiting for the sun to move near our part of the earth again. *'It's too late.'* That was what he'd said.

I had to stay behind after school to help get all last term's art work down from the walls, and by the time I left it was nearly dark. I hurried down to the allotments. It was bitterly cold down there, directly exposed to the moors, and there was very little light left. The town lights were behind me. I picked my way along the path. A stray cat yowled at me from its ratting place near the whitened mound of the compost heap. I found my way by memory to the high bulk of Rab's shed, and I could tell that it was in darkness.

I went up to it all the same, and tried to peer in through that high curtained window. Surely they hadn't gone again so soon? I was just about to move away when I heard a movement inside; a kind of hollow knocking. 'Rab?' I shouted. 'You in there?' There was silence, but then the knocking came again; but it wasn't knocking at all, it was stamping, and I knew the sound from the farmers' yards down in the valley. It was the impatient clopping sound of a horse's hooves. I backed away, and the stamping began again, more urgent this time. The high wooden door of the hut shook, and I knew that the horse inside was rearing up against it, beating its hooves, trying to tear it down.

'Stop it!' I shouted, hardly realising what I was doing. 'I know what you are. You're not a horse at all. You're only a nightmare.'

I started to run, skidding on the slippery path as I went. But how could it be a nightmare, when the lights of my town were blinking like low yellow stars in front of me, and I could hear the drone of cars making for the motorway? Behind me was the thundering of hooves pounding on wood, and the terrible splintering as the door began to give way.

I ran wildly towards the warm familiar town lights, and as the path turned to stubbed grass and then met the pavement I skidded on the ice, fell headlong and closed my eyes, wanting to sleep ...

'All right, love? Come on. Up you get. No bones broken.'

Davey Brown, an old friend of my dad's, hauled me up and brushed me down.

'You're shaking like a plate of jelly. Come on, get in my car, and I'll run you home. I want a word with your dad anyway, about the new allotment hut ... In you get.'

I was glad of his offer. Davey had left the engine running when he stopped to help me up, and the car was still warm.

'Good job I saw you fall,' he said, as we pulled away into the traffic. 'You must have been going at quite a pace to come down like that. Shouldn't run on ice, you know.'

'I saw a horse,' I said. 'It scared me.'

'A horse?'

'I didn't exactly see it,' I added. 'I heard it. On the allotments.'

He shook his head. 'I doubt it. How would a horse get there? Whereabouts on the allotments?'

It felt safer now, in the warmth of the car. It was comforting to be told that I must have imagined it. I didn't mind if he laughed at me. I wanted to be brought away from the nightmare.

'I thought I heard it,' I said, 'in the hut.'

'But there isn't a hut,' Davey said, 'Not any more.'

Not any more. I began to shiver violently again now. Nightmare and reality became one thing, as I walked again in my memory down the dark track, past the cat crouching in the hedge, saw the looming shape of the hut, peered through the window, touched the wood of the door ...

'We pulled it down over the weekend,' Davey went on. 'Real eyesore, that thing. That's why I'm wanting a word with your dad about building us a dry, secure little hut for the allotment users to keep their tools and seeds and things in. We've been wanting one on that site for years ...'

We waited for the traffic lights to change. Was I really in Davey's car, I wondered, or was I still lying on the ice, or peering through the hut window, or chasing Rab over the moors, or looking at the frozen slab of the slab of the Downpour ...

'But it's their home,' I managed to say, trying to get him to talk again. As long as Davey talked, surely I was in the car next to him, safe and warm, and on my way home. 'They live there.'

'Old Ged? He came up a few days ago. He wanted to collect a few bits and pieces that he'd left behind. But he'll not be coming back, he said. Not without the lad. I expect your mum and dad told you, didn't they? Terrible business, that.'

We had arrived at our house. I followed him down the jennel and into the kitchen. Mum sat me down by the radiator and gave me a hot drink and got on with preparing the meal while my dad and Davey worked out a price agreement for the hut they were wanting on the allotments. I went out into the back room while they were talking, and I drew back the heavy curtains and looked out across the dark plain of the moors. Something outside was dripping, very slowly, very softly.

My mother came in and stood beside me.

'Shall I tell you about Rab?' she said.

Dread slowed the pumping of my blood.

'Listen,' I said. 'It's thawing.'

'Yes. The forecast said temperatures would go up tonight.' She touched my arm. 'I thought you and Rab had stopped seeing each other years ago. That's why I didn't tell you.'

'Rab was my best friend,' I said.

I didn't look at her while she was telling me. I didn't listen to her. I knew already what had happened to him. I listened instead to Rab and myself talking quietly together, sitting next to each other on the Edge, the day he showed me the frozen horse.

'*Everything's died.*'

'*The winter solstice. Everything's standing still. The sun, and the grass, and the streams, and the birds. Nothing moving.*'

'*You'd think it was waiting for something.*'

'*There's nothing to wait for now. It's too late.*'

'Rab was killed about three weeks ago,' my mother was saying. 'He stole a ride on somebody's horse, and it took fright and threw him. He died on midwinter's day. The longest night of the year.'

The dripping from the roof had turned into a trickle. I could see it coursing down the outside of the window; ice running free again. Tomorrow the Downpour would crack and burst and gush back to life. But I would never see Rab again. I thought of him, a free spirit, urging the black horse on over the moors, riding free, laughing.

'I already knew that,' I said to her. 'Rab came back to tell me.'

THE SMILE OF
EUGENE RITTER

John Gordon

When Eugene Ritter grasped the handle but was unable
to open the door, he knew what had happened. His
strength had not diminished, but no matter how hard
he tried, he could not make the handle turn, or even
rattle.

Rattle, he thought, was a good word in the circumstances. Death rattle. He had once heard the clatter
in an old man's throat as he lay dying. It had been like
a loose slat caught in a regular gust of wind, and had
become more noisy rather than quieter towards the
end, as if the structure of a whole life had become
unshored and was shaking itself into the ground.

But there was nothing unstable about the room in
which Eugene Ritter found himself. Just the opposite.
He smiled and wondered if anything showed on his face.
It would be interesting to know. He began to move
across the room towards the dressing table, until he
saw that something was draped over the oval mirror
and successfully hid it. All of it.

'How very unfortunate,' he said, well aware that his
disappointment was a pretence. Not being able to open

73

a door was one thing, but to gaze into a mirror and see no reflection would be quite another. 'Much more shattering,' he said, and smiled again, pleased that his sense of humour had remained with him. The mirror test could wait. As one who had so recently become dead, he had to acclimatise himself gradually.

It was reassuring to speak aloud. 'I suppose, technically speaking, I am a ghost,' he said, 'therefore there would be nothing substantial enough to be reflected in a mirror.'

As with a werewolf. The thought crossed his mind only instantly to be thrust out. 'Murderer, perhaps,' he said, 'but werewolf never!'

His exclamation had been loud, and this made him wonder if his voice made any sound that a living ear could detect. But the room was his own bedroom, and there was nobody in it but himself. Not even that awful child. He smiled again. Rebecca had been there at the end and, in a sense, had been responsible for making a ghost of him, but not before he had had his revenge.

'It would be pleasant,' he said, 'to try out my ghostly voice on you, Rebecca, and haunt you and your whining mother.' He smiled at the thought of driving them, terrified and whimpering, from his house. But this would never be. Eugene Ritter had taken his revenge in another way.

He was curious, nevertheless, to know what effect, if any, he had on the world of the living. A thought occurred to him. Sound depended on the movement of air so, if there were some means of detecting a vibration, he could tell whether his spectral voice would be heard by a normal ear. He gazed around him. It was a large room, in a large house, and furnished in a style that still, after all that had happened here, gave him pleasure. There was a faint silvery sheen in the pattern of the wall covering that contrasted admirably with the dark wood and hint of inlaid gilt of the furniture, and enough light came from the three tall windows to show

how widely spaced each piece was, without clutter.

The dimness of one corner was lightened by a vase of silk flowers, and it was towards these he moved. He stooped and blew on their petals. They did not stir. He raised both hands with the idea of carrying the vase nearer a window where he would be able to detect the slightest quiver, but his fingers and palms, although they cupped the shape of the vase, had no sense of touch and were powerless to lift. He tried brushing the flowers, but even though his hand moved with what appeared to be adequate strength to make them bow down, the delicate petals stood motionless. And they remained motionless, no matter how hard he thrust.

He straightened and moved slowly to the centre window to stand, as he often had in life, looking out. The parkland with its islands of trees was absorbing the yellow light of an autumn evening, and nothing stirred. It was exactly as he had perfected it, a landscape without figures. And then his sister had arrived, with her brat.

Eugene Ritter discovered that bitterness had followed him beyond the grave. One moment of sentiment on his part had allowed his grounds, his house, and his life to be invaded. His sister had been absurdly grateful when he had offered her shelter after her husband had died, leaving her with a child but no income. It was to have been a temporary arrangement – except that she, finding herself in the home of her childhood, came to regard it as her right to be there. She had heaved great sighs when he so much as hinted that her claims had lapsed when she married and moved away, and there were tears when he offered help to enable her to establish herself elsewhere. It was no longer her home. Eugene Ritter had made the house his own. She and the child disturbed all the subtleties he had created in his own image. His jaw muscles tightened, as they had done so often during the months when his careful life was being tarnished, and he turned away from the window.

Soon it would be dark. Columns of shadow already stood in the corners of the room and, without thinking of the likely outcome, he crossed to the light switch near the door and pressed it. It did not move, and he was certain that at that moment, if there had been anybody within the house, his sigh would have been heard. It had a depth of feeling that must have carried. But now, when he again spoke aloud, he knew that his words were as valueless as words mouthed under water.

'At least I have my own senses,' he said. It was more than he could have expected. Death was not, after all, oblivion. It was true he had no physical strength, and it was quite possible that he had no physical appearance, yet this very lack could perhaps be turned to his advantage. It must be this absence of material substance that gave the spirits of departed people the ability to dissolve through doors and walls.

He stretched both arms in front of himself and, like a man feeling his way in the dark, approached the door. He would pass through it like a true ghost. He was aware that his palms touched the painted surface, yet the sensation was slight. This was what a ghost must feel as it sank into a solid object, sifting into the crude grains of smooth paint and wood to occupy the same space. He decided that when he was absorbed as far as his eyes, he would pause and look around himself to observe the hidden heart of the door. Life could never offer possession so complete.

Eugene Ritter was anticipating what he would see within the heart of the door when, quite suddenly, he realised that he had stopped walking. He tried to continue but he could not press his limbs forward.

His smile faded. He looked to where his hands should have been submerged in the door, but they were still visible, pressed against the surface. He thrust. His fingers remained in view. He thrust again. There was not even a faint tingle of pressure against his palms. Whatever sensation he had felt earlier had been an illusion.

For the first time, despair swept through him. He turned to face a room in which his loneliness was so complete that he could not vary it by putting even one new wrinkle in the bedclothes or turn a single page in the book at his bedside. The only consolation was that he was able to move within the four walls. He turned from the door and took a pace forward. In that instant Eugene Ritter found that, imprisoned though he was, all was not lost. A single step had taken him into a pleasure so intense he had experienced it only once before.

He was alone no longer. Rebecca was there. The detested child, thirteen years of age, pale and with that sickening desire to please distorting her forlorn face, stood in the middle of the room. He had detested her in life, and he detested her still, but now he was delighted to see her.

He made no attempt to test his voice on her, for there was no need. Her sudden appearance behind him in the room had made him realise what was happening. Of course she was there. Of course she was with him. She had to be, for she also was dead. She had died in this room, and in a moment she had to die again, for that was the way with ghosts. They were condemned to repeat the main anguish of their lives. The only difference was that Rebecca's anguish was Eugene Ritter's moment of greatest joy.

It began to happen. Her expression changed. There was alarm mixed with her pleading. And she spoke.

'Please,' she said.

He heard her, but it was still no proof that there was any sound in the room. One ghost could hear another without a breath being stirred.

'Please can Mummy have the little box?'

Her voice was rather high-pitched for a girl of her

age. She whined, he thought, like her mother. And the sentimental plea to be given the box was her mother's doing. Eugene Ritter gazed at her but said no word.

'The little box.' The girl was fighting her fear of him. 'She just wants to look at it.'

Eugene Ritter saw her point towards the dressing table. *His* dressing table. *His* box. It was a casket for trinkets, of no value, but it had belonged to his mother. Now it was his. His sister should never have sent her child on this errand. He broke his silence.

'Tell your mother,' he said, speaking clearly, 'that I cannot let her have the box. I am using it. It has some of my possessions inside it. Personal things.'

The words were a repetition. He had said them before in replying to the same request, and it would happen again. There was no avoiding it. He and the girl were locked into a performance that would be endlessly repeated. They were ghosts, and, in the manner of ghosts, they could not free themselves from the scene of their own deaths.

'Mummy's crying,' said Rebecca. 'She was thinking about the time when she used to play with the box when she was little, and she wanted me to see it.'

She looked at him with brimming eyes. He was disgusted that she should attempt to win him over with tears. But the girl, as he knew she would, mistook his hesitation for a sign that he was weakening, and she took a step forward. It was a fatal mistake.

'We'll only keep it for a minute,' she said, and reached for the box. It was then that he raised his arm to strike, and she saw it.

'No!' she cried, but Eugene Ritter smiled.

'Don't!'

He saw her face mouth the word, just as it had done that last time. His temper, as it was bound to do, surged again.

'Please don't!'

Eugene Ritter towered over her and struck down.

The hands that tried to stop him were as useless as they had been then. He remembered the pale fingers clutching at his arm, too late and too feeble. Now they were paler and transparent, more ghostlike than he himself. But the sudden jar of the blow was real, and the sensation of the thud as she fell. He had the satisfaction of experiencing it. It came with the thump in his heart.

Eugene Ritter looked down at her where she was sprawled on the floor, utterly still, and he smiled. She was dead. She lay at an awkward angle and she was sickly white. The blow had done more than he intended. He had committed murder, but even in life Eugene Ritter had smiled at that moment. There would be no price for him to pay for her death. The thump in his heart had told him that.

It was over. He was released, but he stooped over to examine her more closely, just as he had done when the body on the floor was real and not, as now, a shadow of itself. But he could not see it. It was just as though, as on that former occasion, the setting sun had once more gleamed in the mirror and dazzled him. He had resented the sudden flare of light, and had picked his dressing gown from the foot of the bed and flung it over the glass.

It had been almost his last moment in life, but now there was no reason to repeat it. The glass was still covered. Whatever had since happened in the room, no one had seen fit to remove it. He did not resent it. He rather welcomed the untidiness. It was evidence of the turmoil he had caused, and the pleasure it had given him. The pleasure of putting an end to the girl, and the pleasure of knowing he had, in a single blow, also struck at her mother. Each dusk would remind him of the intensity of that moment, and the final scene would play itself out again and again.

Greyness had seeped into the room, and with it came a great tiredness. Even that had happened before. He recalled the lethargy that had swept over him a few moments after the girl, for the first time, had thudded to the floor.

How long had it been since it had all happened? He looked around the room. Everything was as he had left it, the dressing gown over the mirror, the bed where he had lain down and died. His heart had given one last great thud and stopped.

Eugene Ritter walked closer to the bed and looked down on it. His body must have lain there some time before they moved him. No doubt they had been more concerned with the girl. There would have been the breathless telephone call, the ambulance siren, the dashing feet, the oxygen mask and the useless heart massage. His sister's panic. All of that while he lay on the bed, the cause of it all, dead but the victor.

The hollow where he had lain still showed in the quilt, and it was time to die again. It was as welcome as sleep. He moved closer and lay down. The hollows of the quilt fitted his limbs and he settled into them, not caring that they had long since lost his warmth. Even his body must have cooled there before they removed him.

The upheaval came in his chest, as he knew it would, and then the blackness before he slowly woke again. It was the middle of the night, and the room was dark in the empty house. He was beyond cold or heat or pain. He was no more than a sensation in the mind, and he was content to stare into the darkness like a corpse until daylight came and then dusk returned and the passion of his hatred renewed him.

The dust of weeks sifted through him, and he lay without thought as the light waxed and waned in the room, emerging from nothingness only at dusk. His need uselessly to explore the room grew less and fell away. The girl was visible to him only in the moments of her fear and her murder. His pleasure did not grow less, and he was content.

THE SMILE OF EUGENE RITTER

The days shortened, and the sun was winking through the bare branches as it put itself to rest on a midwinter afternoon when the handle of the door turned. The door swung slowly open, and the figure of a woman stood within the deeper shadows at the head of the stairs, with the empty darkness of the well of the hall behind her. She moved cautiously forward. The sound of her breathing was louder than her footstep on the carpet or the rustle of her clothes. She was afraid.

Eugene Ritter lay where he was and watched until the pink light of the setting sun fell briefly on her and revealed her face. His sister had returned.

It was then that he rose from the bed and stood in front of her. She shivered, but no more. She did not see him, but nevertheless she moved sideways, away from the bed, and her eyes searched the room.

'It's cold,' she murmured, 'and it'll soon be dark. I should have remembered to have the electricity connected.'

No electricity. He saw her run a finger through the thick dust and comment on it. So the house had been shut up, and for some time. The two funerals must have been long since over. Eugene Ritter watched his sister pulling open drawers, lifting his clothes, pawing them over, examining them.

'I shall have to get rid of all these things,' she said aloud, keeping up her courage in the cold and darkening room. 'The sooner the better. Get rid of him.'

Eugene Ritter longed at that moment to make her suffer, to appear in front of her and frighten her to the brink of death. Death. The thought made him pause. Death. His sister was no stranger to death. Rebecca, her own daughter, had died in this room.

Eugene Ritter smiled. He himself might be invisible but darkness was creeping on and soon he would have a companion. Surely a mother would have eyes to see her own daughter enter the room. And then see her struck down. Eugene Ritter's impatience left him. His revenge would come in its own time.

His sister's tour had taken her across the room to the dressing table. She saw the dressing gown that he had flung across the mirror and she touched it, squeamishly. It slipped down, falling clear of the glass to lie on the floor. She left it, but Eugene Ritter had seen that the slithering movement had caused her to shudder. There would be more for her to shudder at in a moment.

Suddenly she gave a little start and reached forward. 'Mother's trinket box!' Her eyes filled with tears as she picked it up. 'Oh, Rebecca!' she said. And then, louder, 'Rebecca!'

She had called for her dead daughter at the correct moment. The light had almost gone from the room, and the time had come. Her mother called again.

'Rebecca!'

He glanced towards the door. She was there. The ghost girl had obeyed her cue, and Eugene Ritter smiled.

His sister was no longer blind. She saw her daughter and went towards her. 'Oh, Rebecca,' she said and then, stupidly, she held out the trinket box towards the ghost. 'Look what I've found, Rebecca.'

The girl came forward and Eugene Ritter went to meet her. There was fear in her eyes, and her mother saw it, as Eugene Ritter knew she would. And it was useless for her to go forward, as she did now, murmuring stupid words of comfort. 'There now, there now, my darling.'

She put out her arms and appeared to enfold the girl, but Eugene Ritter knew her anguish would at that moment become unbearable. The girl would ignore her, drawn as she must be towards her uncle, who waited to strike her down. While her mother watched.

He was poised to deliver the blow. There was a sob, and for a moment longer the mother's body shielded the girl from him. He heard her say, 'There's nothing more to worry about, Rebecca. It's all over.'

THE SMILE OF EUGENE RITTER

It was not over. Eugene Ritter stepped forward. His sister's body still obscured the girl, but the naked mirror showed him the room. He glanced towards it. He saw his sister within it, and her daughter. She had not yet realised she was embracing a ghost.

'I saw him on the bed.' It was Rebecca's voice. 'When I woke up I was on the floor, and he was there.'

In the mirror Eugene Ritter saw the girl, still within her mother's arms, point towards the bed.

'I crawled away,' she sobbed. 'I left him.'

She could not have crawled away. Eugene Ritter had seen her lying dead on the carpet. He glanced at her again in the mirror, and as he did so the truth began to dawn. She had survived. That was why her image showed in the glass. She had woken up, and she had crawled away.

'We should never have come here, Rebecca.' Her mother, comforting her, led her to the door. 'We'll never come back – ever.'

There had been no murder. Eugene Ritter knew now that at the moment of his own death he had, in his passion, deluded himself into believing the girl to be dead. It was the last memory of his life and it was repeating itself over and over.

He saw Rebecca and her mother go through the doorway together. As the door closed behind them, he moved forward until he stood in the spot where the girl had fallen. Surely the act itself would remain. Even if it was a delusion, he would be able to conjure up the shadow of the girl, as he had succeeded in doing, night after night. The satisfaction would repeat itself.

The footsteps of Rebecca and her mother faded as they moved down the stairs and across the dark hall. Listening, he heard the distant thud of the outer door. Then silence.

They had gone, but they could not rob him of his ghostly pleasures. Eugene Ritter leant forward to smile at himself in the mirror. The utter emptiness of the room forced itself upon him. He saw the carpet on which he stood, and the bed behind him, but of himself there was no trace. Nor of the girl. Nor would there ever be. She had exorcised herself from his mind, and would never return. The room had become no more than his prison.

He remained where he was, gazing into the oval glass. The mirror gaped and gathered shadows, but there was nothing to show Eugene Ritter that his smile was dying away.

EFFLORESCENCE

Jan Mark

I don't suppose the tunnel is there any more. It ran under a stretch of disused railway line and the last time I visited the town, about twenty years ago, there was earth-moving equipment at work in the meadow beyond it, and already a row of houses at the end of the footpath. Probably the foopath is a street by now, and no street would have fitted into that tunnel; it was only six feet across. No, I should guess that the old line has gone and the tunnel with it. This may be just as well.

Dennis Willis and I used to walk through the tunnel twice a day, five days a week, on our way to school and back. My school was Coldharbour High; Dennis went to St Augustine's R.C. For a long while this didn't matter, but at the beginning of our second year Dennis's twin brothers started at the infant school and Dennis had to escort them there. Dennis thought this was unfair. I thought it was criminally stupid, like asking your pet baa-lamb to take the mastiffs for a walk; not that Raymond and David were actively carnivorous. They did not hurl themselves at passers-by and gnaw their ankles, they went in more for what is known

as structural damage: gate-posts, bird-baths, windows.
Rose bushes and milk bottles were not safe either in
their vicinity. In those days the footpath ran alongside
a row of cottages with very small unfenced front
gardens, where the milk bottles and rose bushes were
within easy reach. Dennis had his work cut out.

The upshot of all this was that Dennis had to leave
home much earlier than before in order to deliver the
twins to the very doorstep of their school because they
could not be trusted to walk even the last hundred
yards on their own. Once or twice I tried leaving early
as well, to give Dennis moral support – and numerical
parity, as Dennis would have it – but there were six of
us at home, all leaving for various schools and jobs,
and in the end I gave up because I was the youngest
and always got trampled in the rush for the bathroom.
All the others had not only to wash but to shave, except
for my mother, of course. I saw less of Dennis on the
way home, too. St Augustine's came out fifteen minutes
before we did. In the good old days, BT (Before Twins),
Dennis used to wait for me by the allotments, where
the town end of the tunnel began, but now the extra
fifteen minutes were taken up with collecting Raymond
and David and somehow we usually managed to miss
each other.

I'm not implying that I used to hide, mind you, and
we still met in the evenings when it was fine or we
didn't have too much homework. Arranging these meet-
ings was a problem as neither of us had a phone, until
Dennis discovered the loose brick. It was probably one
of the twins who discovered it or more likely loosened
it himself. Given time, no doubt, they would have demol-
ished the entire tunnel, but this particular brick was
on the edge, at the allotments' end, and could be lifted
right out. Dennis's idea was that if one us wanted to
communicate with the other he should leave a message
on a piece of paper shoved in behind the brick. Each of
us would check, as we went through the tunnel, to see

if there were anything in the hole.

This worked for about a week until someone else discovered the loose brick. The someone else was Godfrey Rains, and he forged a message from Dennis for me to find on the way to school. Then he forged another one from me, which he left for Dennis the same evening. They were identical. 'See you round by the privet bush, back of the pub. 7.30.' Our writing was easy to forge as we, and Godfrey, had attended the same primary school, taught to write, as our parents had been, by ancient Miss Babbington, who had herself been taught to write, so rumour had it, by the author of Genesis. When we rendezvoused innocently under the privet bush at the back of the Three Choughs, we were fallen upon by the Rains brothers, Peter Hold-stock and Robert Gann. It was clear that we would have to think of something more secret than a loose brick.

This was not so easy, partly because the brick had seemed perfect and once you have enjoyed perfection anything else is bound to feel a bit of a let-down. Also, there really *was* nowhere else that would serve as a hiding place. What we needed was the kind of thing that spies use for a dead letter drop; a telephone box, litter bin, hollow tree, post hole, but there was nothing. Dennis and I lived on opposite sides of the estate; our routes converged only at the footpath, which started out running between two chain-link fences and then lay across the meadow past the terraced row of afore-mentioned cottages with their gardens that had neither fences nor hedges. In case you think that this doesn't sound very cottagey, they weren't thatched country cottages with roses round the door and wall-to-wall holly-hocks; they had been built as railwaymen's dwellings in much the same style as the station only plainer, without any fancy woodwork.

The third problem was that the Rains Gang were now onto us, watching out for what Dennis called 'clandestine correspondence.'

'What we need is a code,' Dennis said. 'Something fantastically complex to mislead the uninitiated.'

'The what?'

'The Rainses,' Dennis said.

'It needn't be *that* complex, then,' I said.

'OK, but it's got to be misleading,' said Dennis. 'It's got to be so misleading that even if they copy it down and show it to someone intelligent, they won't be able to crack it.'

'Oh, that sort of code,' I said. I was in the Scouts at the time, which Dennis was not, and I'd been thinking along the lines of knotted grass stems, bent twigs, circles of stones. I said as much. Dennis's face became pinched with scorn.

'How long do you think that kind of sign would last?' he demanded. 'The Rains Mob would kick it to *fragments*. That's what they're good at. Why do you think Newt Patrol never gets back to base when you're out tracking?'

'I'm in Beaver Patrol,' I said with dignity, for Dennis, I knew, thought little of Scouting for Boys. 'There isn't a Newt Patrol.'

'You exasperate me,' Dennis said. 'Give me a week to cogitate.'

I noticed that he didn't imagine that I should be able to come up with something inside a week. Without doubt I did exasperate him. (Dennis is now Brother Dennis of that silent Cistercian order commonly known as Trappists, which seems a terrible waste of a huge vocabulary.)

As it happened, it was a week to the day before Dennis and I ran into each other again, in the tunnel, on the way home from school. Dennis was there already, but I guessed that long before I saw him, because as I came through the allotments I could see Raymond and David trying to impale each other on the railings that were meant to keep unauthorised persons off the embankment and away from the little black hut on the top of it, alongside the permanent way, where, legend had it, a railwayman had frozen to death during a blizzard in the middle of the last century. Such huts had little brick chimneys and looked enticingly cosy, but knowing what had happened in this one made it seem less cosy.

Raymond and David had no designs on the hut; they were occupied with the railings. There was something uncannily prehensile in the way they went up and down those railings which made me wonder if there wasn't perhaps an orang-utan a couple of generations back in the Willis family, absent-mindedly converted by missionaries. Dennis himself had long arms and rather short legs.

Dennis was under the archway with a stick of chalk, writing something on the brickwork at head height. He didn't hear me approach, owing to his ululating brothers, so I stood behind him and tried to read what he had written.

J TYF BE AE BBO AEIO R SIAOIAEAPQVBXYZ As I watched he added, AJJOAOIU BST SO I FIAO GGT GOAT

'Goat?' I said. Dennis jumped, spun round and grinned.

'Goat,' he said, 'or toad, or deer, or seal, or – '

'Sheep?' I said.

'Not sheep.'

'Newt?'

'No.'

'Tyrannosaurus Rex?'

'No,' said Dennis, 'but boot or suit or bean or soil. *Come down off of that!*' he roared suddenly, as he finally noticed what the twins were up to. 'Look, I'll come round yours this evening and show you – no I won't. I'll meet you.'

'Where?'

Dennis pointed to his row of letters, chalked on the

brickwork. 'Where it says; by the phone box.'

'That says, "I'll meet you by the phone box"?'

'It says,' Dennis explained patiently, 'Tonight, 6.30, phone box.'

'All that says "Tonight, 6.30, phone box"? Isn't there a shorter way?'

Dennis looked hurt. 'This is Rains-proof, at least, I hope it is. Tonight will reveal all.'

'What about the goat?'

'Forget the goat,' Dennis said. 'It could just as easily be a boil.'

The phone box was the only one on the estate, nearer to my house than to Dennis's, and it was very rarely working. But it was a place where everybody met, or hung around on the off-chance of a meeting. It was said of the phone box that if you stood there long enough everyone you knew would go past eventually. This being the case, it was also pretty safe. Even the Rains Gang was not foolhardy enough to attempt a frontal attack or even an outflanking manoeuvre, because at least one of my very big brothers was likely to be there, or all three of them.

I set out at 6.25, convinced that either Dennis was onto something good or else was off his trolley. He just looked smug, though, when I spotted him sitting on the remains of the bench, by the remains of the litter bin, and ignoring the shuffling and snogging that went on all around him. When he saw me he got up and I saw he was carrying an exercise book. I was in for a period of instruction.

'Where shall we go?' I said.

'Back to yours?' he suggested.

'Well, you could have come round mine anyway,' I said, crossly. 'You needn't have hauled me out here.'

'Ah,' said Dennis, 'but I told you, didn't I, we had to see if it was Rains-proof.'

I looked around. There were no Rainses about.

'It could take *them* a week to decipher it if you just wrote it out backwards.'

'Never underestimate your adversary,' Dennis said, darkly, 'or as you and I might put it: the Rains Gang may not be as thick as we think.'

We walked back to my house rapidly, because I was in a hurry to find out how the code worked and Dennis was dying to tell me. Also, I was only too aware that even if the Rainses hadn't cracked it, neither had I. Indoors we sat at the table and Dennis opened his book. There was the tantalizing message again.

JTYFBEAEBBOAEIORSIAOIAEAPQVBXYZAJJO
AOIUBSTSOIFIAOGGTGOAT

'Got it yet?' Dennis asked, after I had studied it for a few minutes.

'Almost,' I lied. Dennis smiled silently and said, 'Here's the misleading bit. This says exactly the same,' and he wrote:

LPTJROEASMIUIUIDPOIIUEOASFXPBNJOLSAE
AOIRNCCEIJOAEMPKBOIL

'Said it could just as easily be a boil,' Dennis murmured.

'That says the same? "Tonight, 6.30, phone box"?'

'Or,' said Dennis, 'KSVCRO -'

'All right!' I yelled. 'I give in. How's it done?'

'It's done,' said Dennis, 'on bricks.'

'Bricks?'

'Remember where I was writing it?'

'In the tunnel.'

'On the bricks,' Dennis said. 'It only works on the bricks. That's the misleading part.' I gawped at him. 'Look, when I wrote it in the tunnel it looked like this, didn't it?' He pointed to the first string of letters.

'Almost,' I said again, but this time I meant it. There *was* a difference. 'There were gaps.'

'Like this?' Dennis wrote again:

J TYF BE EA BBO AEIO R SIAOI AEAPQ VBXYZ
AJJO AOIU BST SO I FIAO GGT GOAT

'Not quite. Some of those words ran together.'

'They only looked as if they did,' Dennis said. 'I wrote one word on each brick, so of course the four and five-letter words seemed to run together. What you saw in the tunnel was:

J TYF BE AE BBO AEIO R SIAOIAEAPQ-
VBXYZAJJOAOIU BST SO I FIAO GGT GOAT

'This – ' he pointed to the previous line, 'is what it really says.' He added, 'You're not going to get it, are you?'

'No,' I admitted, and then I suddenly saw what he had done. 'Hang on!' I wrote: IOU LBW AAA

'Let's hope it never comes to that,' Dennis said. I think he was slightly sorry that I had worked out the code, but he *had* given me a lot of help. We shook hands solemnly.

'Give it a few more days,' Dennis said. 'We'll write up another test piece and if the Rainses still don't get it, we'll put it into production.'

What Dennis wrote in the tunnel read, brick for brick: WHO GMT LEA EARO USA I BEST OMO AT EE TO UEO OU AAA IP UFO IN Z which, had Godfrey Rains been able to translate it, would have brought the gang down on us like Atilla and the Huns, since it actually said, GODFREY RAINS IS A RAT. I'd been practising at home, so when I passed under the railway arch and saw Dennis's message strung out along a course of brickwork, I could read it almost without hesitating, but then, I knew the brick trick. When I came home that evening, Godfrey himself and Robert Gann were standing staring at it.

'This yours?' Godfrey said, moving to block my path.

'Nah.' I joined in the staring. 'WHOGMTLEAE-AROUSAIBESTOMO ... I best Omo? *Pufoinz?* It's a code, innit?'

Robert was copying it down on the back of his hand, but although I knew it was unlikely to get washed off, I could see that there was little chance of his deciphering it before wind and rain faded it away. WHOGMTLEAEARO ... he printed, laboriously. Godfrey, meanwhile, tried to erase it in the hope of spoiling somebody's fun, but chalk is harder to wipe from brick than almost anything else. Dennis's code was definitely Rains-proof.

When, after a week, we still hadn't been beaten to pulp, we put the code into operation. It wasn't merely Rains-proof, it was everybody-proof, that infuriating combination of real words, initials, acronyms and meaningless groups of letters. Sometimes a frustrated would-be cryptographer vented his spleen by interfering with our messages, but we could always spot an altered letter and imitations were nonsense – up until just before half-term, that is. I remember the date exactly.

To foil imitators we had taken to ending messages with the date, and it was always the first thing I checked. As the days shortened it was so dim in the tunnel by home-time that I now carried a torch, and I had to look carefully for today's message, for by now the tunnel looked as if someone had sprayed it with alphabet soup; we had begun to write over our old white messages in red or blue chalk. I stood in the hollow darkness skimming the walls for the signal, which would be that day's date. I couldn't find it, and I was just coming to the conclusion that Dennis had written nothing that day when I noticed, far up in the arch of the tunnel, a row of marks, higher than any of us could reach. I read them with ease.

LLLII LII IL LILL III

Now, according to our code, that did actually say something, and my first reaction was fury that at last someone had cracked it. Then I began to wonder; we had never done it using only two letters although that, as this proved, was perfectly possible, and the ones used here are about the simplest letters there are. Not even a baby would have had much trouble with I and L; not

even a Rains. I also wondered who on earth would go
to all the trouble of climbing up to write on the very
top of the arch – climbing up on what? Shoulders? The
arch was about ten feet high. I had a vision of the Rains
Gang, lightweight Godfrey perched on taller Robert or
fat brother Desmond, falteringly tracing those simple
letters in haste before his scaffolding collapsed. I felt
betrayed – and nervous.

There was no need to write down the message; once
I knew what it said I could easily re-encode it, and next
morning I went round to Dennis's house and wrote it
out for him.

'Someone's on to us, Den,' I said.

Dennis, refusing to panic, looked at what I had
written. He said, 'On the roof of the arch, you
say?'

'Right at the top of the curve.'

'Depends which way round you look at it from,'
Dennis said. He turned the paper round. 'It could
say, "One thousand, one hundred and seventeen billion … " ' he was good at maths too, ' "seven hundred
and seventeen million … " '

'Come off it, Willis,' I snapped. 'That says eight days.
You know it does.'

'Funny sort of message,' Dennis said. 'Eight days of
what?'

'Eight days *to* what?'

'To the end of the month?'

'Hallowe'en,' I said.

Dennis counted. 'Thirty days hath September, April,
June. … You're right.' He looked at me uncomfortably.
'Someone's mucking about.'

'Yes, and they're mucking about with our code.'

'Let's go and look,' said Dennis.

It was dark in the tunnel even in summer. Now,
halfway through a dull autumn morning, it was gloomy,
but we had the torch. I flashed it up into the tunnel's
vault. The letters had faded a little, it seemed to me,

94

since yesterday afternoon, but I hardly noticed that. Below them, on the next course but one, was a second set.

LLIII LII IL LILL III

'That doesn't say one trillion anything,' I said.

'Seven days,' Dennis muttered. He read the letters aloud, 'Lliiiliiillilliii,' a nasty gibbering whine.

'Shut up,' I said, not liking it at all. 'Someone *is* mucking about.'

'That's not chalk,' Dennis said. 'It's not written in chalk.'

'You can't tell from here.'

'Bend down,' said Dennis.

'What for?'

'So I can stand on your shoulders.'

'You're a stone heavier than I am,' I said. 'You bend down.'

Dennis crouched. I climbed onto his shoulders and balanced myself against the wall as Dennis slowly straightened up. Idiotic words slid past my eyes as I rose: GGA ... OSP ... GRAW ... OOOI ... MARB ... ULP ... Dennis turned gingerly and I braced my hands against the curve of the roof.

'Can you see anything?' Dennis said.

I reached out cautiously and touched today's letters, LLIII ... 'It's not chalk.' The marks were white, but a blue-white, like crystals, and when I touched them a faint crust crumbled under my finger, leaving the marks on the bricks. 'It's more like salt.'

'Efflorescence,' Dennis said, predictably. He teetered and I fell off.

'Fluorescence?'

'Efflorescence. Salts coming to the surface in brick-work – well, not just in brickwork; stones, breezeblocks, even.'

'You mean it's just chance, those marks?' I'd skinned my knee.

'Damn funny chance,' Dennis growled, wiping my

boot prints from his shoulders. We stood looking up at the letters.

'Could be coincidence,' I said. Dennis glared; I was pinching one of his long words. Dennis was definitely Holmes. I was only Watson.

'Coincidence, my foot,' said Dennis. 'Those marks weren't put *on* the brick – they came out of it.'

'You mean, we called them out?'

We were both staring at those lines and lines of letters.

'One thousand, one hundred and seventeen billion billion, seven hundred and seventeen billion, seven hundred and eleven million, one hundred and seventy-one thousand, one hundred and seventeen,' Dennis droned.

The next day was Sunday but I went down to the tunnel, just to check. There was a third line of letters: LIIII LII IL LILL III

Six days.

Each line was lower than the last. By the time it had reached IILLL LII IL LILL III, two days, whatever *it* was, the words were about seven feet from the ground. You could see that in two days time they would be at shoulder level – an adult's shoulder, that is. On the morning of the thirty-first, which was a Saturday, Dennis and I met by prior arrangement (the usual prior arrangement; we refused to be scared off) and went along to the tunnel to see what was there. The inscriptions of the last week seemed to flow faintly above us in the vault, from the almost illegible LLLII LII IL LILL III down to yesterday's, still sharp and clear: ILLLL LII IL LILL; one day.

We looked everywhere, but there was nothing else written that hadn't been put there by us or our envious imitators, in chalk. We decided not to go through the tunnel again until Monday.

That night Mum, Dad and my three brothers went to

a Hallowe'en party on the other side of town, a grown-up affair with drink; nothing in it for me. I could have gone with them, but Dennis's mum said I might stay at theirs, and the two of us sat up half the night cogitating (Dennis, of course) on what might be happening in the tunnel. We were almost tempted to go out and look, and were almost glad that Dennis's mother forbade us going anywhere.

When I went home next morning the house was in an uproar. It had been a very cold night all over the region, but in our house the temperature must have hit fifteen below. The garden was white with rime and every chrysanthemum, dahlia and late-flowering rose was blighted and black. The windows were thick with frost ferns and indoors the pipes had frozen. People rushed about murmuring of freak weather conditions and fires were lit, whereupon the pipes, which had burst, thawed dramatically. Plumbers were called. Gradually the house warmed up, but not before I had been into my bedroom. I have never known such cold; it took the breath away, that, and the curious marks in the ice on the window:
L LLL LI II LLI IIII L

Tonight.

Neither of us ever went through the tunnel again. If it is still there I doubt if I would go through it even now. Even twenty years on it would seem like putting my luck at risk, and there were several elements of luck in the whole affair. I consider that I had a very lucky escape, although it was several weeks before I had another good night's sleep. It was luck, too, that our correspondent didn't go to Dennis's house, which he might well have done, considering it was Dennis's code that fetched him. Dennis didn't say much when I told him what had happened, but I can't help wondering if that didn't have something to do with his abandoning the idea of becoming a cryptographer and entering a monastery instead. I never spoke of it to anyone else although, much later, I asked my dad in a casual way if he knew anything about the railwayman who was alleged to have died in that little black shack beside the permanent way, just beyond the tunnel. 'He was a telegraphist,' said Dad. 'You know, dot-dot-dot-dash,' and he tapped on the table with bunched fingers, operating an imaginary buzzer. So it was sheer *bad* luck, obviously, that there should be someone using the tunnel who was not misled by Dennis's version of the Morse Code.

Note You need to know Morse Code to decypher the messages. As a clue, IOU LBW AAA equals the familiar ... --- ... (SOS). Go on from there.

BANG, BANG – WHO'S DEAD?

Jane Gardam

There is an old house in Kent not far from the sea where a little ghost girl plays in the garden. She wears the same clothes winter and summer – long black stockings, a white dress with a pinafore, and her hair flying about without a hat, but she never seems either hot or cold. They say she was a child of the house who was run over at the drive gates, for the road outside is on an upward bend as you come to the gates of The Elms – that's the name of the house, The Elms – and very dangerous. But there were no motor cars when children wore clothes like that and so the story must be rubbish.

No grown person has ever seen the child. Only other children see her. For over fifty years, when children have visited this garden and gone off to play in it, down the avenue of trees, into the walled rose-garden, or down deep under the high dark caves of the polished shrubs where queer things scutter and scrattle about on quick legs and eyes look out at you from round corners, and pheasants send up great alarm calls like rattles, and whirr off out of the wet hard bracken right under your nose, 'Where've you been?' they get asked when they get back to the house.

'Playing with that girl in the garden.'

'What girl? There's no girl here. This house has no children in it.'

'Yes it has. There's a girl in the garden. She can't half run.'

When last year The Elms came up for sale, two parents – the parents of a girl called Fran – looked at each other with a great longing gaze. The Elms.

'We could never afford it.'

'I don't know. It's in poor condition. We might. They daren't ask much for such an overgrown place.'

'All that garden. We'd never be able to manage it. And the house is so far from anywhere.'

'It's mostly woodland. It looks after itself.'

'Don't you believe it. Those elms would all have to come down for a start. They're diseased. There's masses of re-planting and clearing to do. And think of the upkeep of that long drive.'

'It's a beautiful house. And not really a huge one.'

'And would you *want* to live in a house with – '

They both looked at Fran who had never heard of the house. 'With what?' she asked.

'Is it haunted?' she asked. She knew things before you ever said them, did Fran. Almost before you thought them.

'Of course not,' said her father.

'Yes,' said her mother.

Fran gave a squealing shudder.

'Now you've done it,' said her father. 'No point now in even going to look at it.'

'How is it haunted?' asked Fran.

'It's only the garden,' said her mother. 'And very *nicely* haunted. By a girl about your age in black stockings and a pinafore.'

'What's a pinafore?'

'Apron.'

'*Apron*. How cruddy.'

'She's from the olden days.'

'Fuddy-duddy-cruddy,' said Fran, preening herself about in her tee-shirt and jeans.

After a while though she noticed that her parents were still rattling on about The Elms. There would be spurts of talk and then long silences. They would stand for ages moving things pointlessly about on the kitchen table, drying up the same plate three times. Gazing out of windows. In the middle of Fran's telling them something about her life at school they would say suddenly, 'Rats. I expect it's overrun with rats.'

Or, 'What about the roof?'

Or, 'I expect some millionaire will buy it for a Country Club. Oh, it's far beyond us, you know.'

'When are we going to look at it?' asked Fran after several days of this, and both parents turned to her with faraway eyes.

'I want to see this girl in the garden,' said Fran because it was a bright sunny morning and the radio was playing loud and children not of the olden days were in the street outside, hurling themselves about on bikes and wearing jeans and tee-shirts like her own and shouting out 'Bang, bang, you're dead.'

'Well, I suppose we could just telephone,' said her mother. 'Make an appointment.'

Then electricity went flying about the kitchen and her father began to sing.

They stopped the car for a moment inside the propped-back iron gates where there stood a rickety table with a box on it labelled 'Entrance Fee. One pound.'

'We don't pay an entrance fee,' said Fran's father. 'We're here on business.'

'When I came here as a child,' said Fran's mother, 'we always threw some money in.'

'Did you often come?'

'Oh, once or twice. Well yes. Quite often. Whenever we had visitors we always brought them to The Elms.

We used to tell them about – '

'Oh yes. Ha-ha. The ghost.'

'Well, it was just something to do with people. On a visit. I'd not be surprised if the people in the house made up the ghost just to get people to come.'

The car ground along the silent drive. The drive curved round and round. Along and along. A young deer leapt from one side of it to the other in the green shadow, its eyes like lighted grapes. Water in a pool in front of the house came into view.

The house held light from the water. It was a long, low, creamy-coloured house covered with trellis and on the trellis pale wisteria, pale clematis, large papery early roses. A huge man was staring from the ground-floor window.

'Is that the ghost?' asked Fran.

Her father sagely, solemnly parked the car. The air in the garden for a moment seemed to stir, the colours to fade. Fran's mother looked up at the gentle old house.

'Oh – look,' she said, 'it's a portrait. Of a man. He seems to be looking out. It's just a painting, for goodness sake.'

But the face of the long-dead eighteenth-century man eyed the terrace, the semi-circular flight of steps, the family of three looking up at him beside their motor-car.

'It's just a painting.'

'Do we ring the bell? At the front door?'

The half-glassed front door above the staircase of stone seemed the door of another shadowy world.

'I don't want to go in,' said Fran. 'I'll stay here.'

'Look, if we're going to buy this house,' said her father, 'you must come and look at it.'

'I want to go in the garden,' said Fran. 'Anyone can see the house is going to be all right.'

All three surveyed the pretty house. Along the top floor of it were heavily-barred windows.

'They barred the windows long ago,' said Fran's

mother, 'to stop the children falling out. The children lived upstairs. Every evening they were allowed to come down and see their parents for half an hour and then they went back up there to bed. It was the custom for children.'

'Did the ghost girl do that?'

'Don't be ridiculous,' said Fran's father.

'But did she?'

'What ghost girl?' said Fran's father. 'Shut up and come and let's look at the house.'

A man and a woman were standing at the end of the hall as the family rang the bell. They were there waiting, looking rather vague and thin. Fran could feel a sort of sadness and anxiety through the glass of the great door, the woman with her gaunt old face just standing; the man blinking.

In the beautiful stone hall at the foot of the stairs the owners and the parents and Fran confronted each other. Then the four grown people advanced with their hands outstretched, like some old dance.

'The house has always been in my family,' said the woman. 'For two hundred years.'

'Can I go out?' asked Fran.

'For over fifty years it was in the possession of three sisters. My three great-aunts.'

'Mum – can I? I'll stay by the car.'

'They never married. They adored the house. They scarcely ever left it or had people to stay. There were never any children in this house.'

'Mum – '

'*Do*,' said the woman to Fran. 'Do go and look around the garden. Perfectly safe. Far from the road.'

The four adults walked away down the stone passage. A door to the dining-room was opened. 'This,' said the woman, 'is said to be the most beautiful dining-room in Kent.'

'What was that?' asked Fran's mother. 'Where is Fran?'

But Fran seemed happy. All four watched her in her white tee-shirt running across the grass. They watched her through the dining-room window all decorated round with frills and garlands of wisteria. 'What a sweet girl,' said the woman. The man cleared his throat and went wandering away.

'I think it's because there have never been any children in this house that it's in such beautiful condition,' said the woman. 'Nobody has ever been unkind to it.'

'I wouldn't say,' said Fran's mother, 'that children were – '

'Oh, but you can tell a house where children have taken charge. Now your dear little girl would never – '

The parents were taken into a room that smelled of rose-petals. A cherry-wood fire was burning although the day was very hot. Most of the fire was soft white ash. Somebody had been doing some needlework. Dogs slept quietly on a rug. 'Oh, Fran would love – ', said Fran's mother looking out of the window again. But Fran was not to be seen.

'Big family?' asked the old man suddenly.

'No. Just – Just one daughter, Fran.'

'Big house for just one child.'

'But you said there had never been children in this house.'

'Oh – wouldn't say never. Wouldn't say never.'

Fran had wandered away towards the garden but then had come in again to the stone hall, where she stopped to look at herself in a long dim glass. There was a blue jar with a lid on a low table, and she lifted the lid and saw a heap of dried rose-petals. The lid dropped back rather hard and wobbled on the jar as if to fall off. 'Children are unkind to houses'; she heard the floating voice of the woman shepherding her parents from one room to another. Fran pulled an unkind face at the jar.

She turned a corner of the hall and saw the staircase sweeping upwards and round a corner too. On the landing someone seemed to be standing, but then as she looked seemed not to be there after all. 'Oh yes,' she heard the woman's voice, 'oh yes, I suppose so. Lovely for children. The old nurseries should be very adequate. We never go up there.'

'If there are nurseries,' said Fran's father, 'there must once have been children.'

'I suppose so. Once. It's not a thing we ever think about.'

'But if it has always been in your family it must have been inherited by children?'

'Oh cousins. Generally cousins inherited. Quite strange how children have not been actually born here.' Fran, who was sitting outside on the steps now in front of the open door, heard the little group of grown-ups clatter off along the stone pavement to the kitchens and thought, 'Why are they going on about children so?'

She thought, 'When they come back I'll go with them. I'll ask to see that painted man down the passage. I'd rather be with Mum to see him close.'

Silence had fallen. The house behind her was still, the garden in front of her stiller. It was the moment in an English early-summer afternoon when there is a pause for sleep. Even the birds stopped singing. Tired by their almost non-stop territorial squawks and cheeps and trills since dawn, they declare a truce and sit still upon branches, stand with heads cocked listening, scamper now and then in the bushes across dead leaves. When Fran listened very hard she thought she could just hear the swish of the road, or perhaps the sea. The smell of the early roses was very strong. Somewhere upstairs a window was opened and a light voice came and went as people moved from room to room. 'Must have gone up the back stairs,' Fran thought and leaned her head against the fluted column of the portico. It was strange. She felt she knew what the house looked like upstairs. Had she been upstairs yet or was she still thinking of going? Going. Going to sleep. Silly.

She jumped up and said, 'You can't catch me. Bang, bang – you're dead.'

She didn't know what she meant by it so she said it again out loud. 'Bang, bang. You're dead.'

She looked at the garden, all the way round from her left to her right. Nothing stirred. Not from the point where a high wall stood with a flint arch in it, not on the circular terrace with the round pond, not in the circle of green with the round gap in it where the courtyard opened to the long drive, and where their car was standing. The car made her feel safe.

Slowly round went her look, right across to where the stone urns on the right showed a mossy path behind them. Along the path, out of the shadow of the house, sun was blazing and you could see bright flowers.

Fran walked to the other side of the round pond and looked up at the house from the courtyard and saw the portrait again looking out at her. It must be hanging in a very narrow passage, she thought, to be so near to the glass. The man was in some sort of uniform. You could see gold on his shoulders and lace on his cuffs. You could see long curls falling over his shoulders. Fancy soldiers with long curls hanging over their uniform. Think of the dandruff.

'Olden days,' said Fran, 'bang, bang, you're dead,' and she set off at a run between the stone urns and in to the flower garden. 'I'll run right round the house,' she thought. 'I'll run like mad. Then I'll say I've been all round the garden all by myself, and not seen the ghost.'

She ran like the wind all round, leaping the flower-beds, tearing along a showering rose-border, here and there, up and down, flying through another door in a stone wall among greenhouses and sheds and old stables, out again past a rose-red dove-house with the doves like fat pearls set in some of the little holes, and others stepping about the grass. Non-stop, non-stop she ran, across the lawn, right turn through a yew hedge, through the flint arch at last and back to the courtyard. 'Oh yes,' she would say to her friends on their bikes. 'I did. I've been there. I've been all round the garden by myself and I didn't see a living soul.'

'A *living* soul.'

'I didn't see any ghost. Never even thought of one.'

'You're brave, Fran. I'd never be brave like that. Are your parents going to buy the house?'

'Don't suppose so. It's very boring. They've never had any children in it. Like an old-folks home. Not even haunted.'

Picking a draggle of purple wisteria off the courtyard wall – and pulling rather a big trail of it down as she did so – Fran began to do the next brave thing: to *walk* round the house. Slowly. She pulled a few petals of the wisteria and gave a carefree sort of wave at the portrait in the window. In front of it, looking out of the window, stood a little girl.

Then she was gone.

For less than a flick of a second Fran went cold round the back of the neck. Then hot.

Then she realised she must be going loopy. The girl hadn't been in a pinafore and frilly dress and long loose hair. She'd been in a white tee-shirt like Fran's own. She had been Fran's own reflection for a moment in the glass of the portrait.

'Stupid. Loopy,' said Fran, picking off petals and scattering them down the mossy path, then along the rosy flagstones of the rose-garden. Her heart was beating very hard. It was almost pleasant, the fright and then the relief coming so close together.

'Well, I thought I saw the ghost but it was only myself reflected in a window,' she'd say to the friends in the road at home.

'Oh Fran, you are brave.'

'How d'you know it was you? Did you see its face? Everyone wears tee-shirts.'

'Oh, I expect it was me all right. They said there'd never been any children in the house.'

'What a cruddy house. I'll bet it's not true. I'll bet there's a girl they're keeping in there somewhere. Behind those bars. I bet she's being imprisoned. I bet they're kidnappers.'

'They wouldn't be showing people over the house and trying to sell it if they were kidnappers. Not while the kidnapping was actually going on, anyway. No, you can tell – ', Fran was explaining away, pulling off the petals. 'There wasn't anyone there but me.' She looked up at the windows in the stable-block she was passing. They were partly covered with creeper, but one of them stood open and a girl in a tee-shirt was sitting in it, watching Fran.

This time she didn't vanish. Her shiny short hair and white shirt shone out clear. Across her humped-up knees lay a comic. She was very much the present day.

'It's you again,' she said.

She was so ordinary that Fran's heart did not begin to thump at all. She thought, 'It must be the gardener's daughter. They must live over the stables and she's just been in the house. I'll bet she wasn't meant to. That's why she ducked away.'

'I saw you in the house,' Fran said. 'I thought you were a reflection of me.'

'Reflection?'

'In the picture.'

The girl looked disdainful. 'When you've been in the house as long as I have,' she said, 'let's hope you'll know a bit more. Oil paintings don't give off reflections. They're not covered in glass.'

'We won't be keeping the oil paintings,' said Fran grandly. 'I'm not interested in things like that.'

'I wasn't at first,' said the girl. 'D'you want to come

108

up? You can climb over the creeper if you like. It's cool up here.'

'No thanks. We'll have to go soon. They'll wonder where I am when they see I'm not waiting by the car.'

'Car?' said the girl. 'Did you come in a car?'

'Of course we came in a car.' She felt furious suddenly. The girl was looking at her oddly, maybe as if she wasn't rich enough to have a car. Just because she lived at The Elms. And she was only the gardener's daughter anyway. Who did she think she was?

'Of course we're going home by car.'

'Well take care on the turn-out to the road then. It's a dangerous curve. It's much too hot to go driving today.'

'I'm not hot,' said Fran.

'You ought to be,' said the girl in the tee-shirt, 'with all that hair and those awful black stockings.'

THE ROAD HOME

Jean Richardson

Gran was not keen on Susan buying a car. She was inclined to be over-protective, and she thought Susan was much too young to be flying up and down motorways, especially late at night. But Susan was old enough – just – to get a licence, and by the time she'd passed her driving test she was old enough to spend the money too.

The money was looked after by Mr Graf, who had invested it in safe securities. He explained to Susan that she would be wise to spend only the interest and leave her capital invested. That way, he said, trying to find words that might mean more to her, she would have a financial safety-net that could last a lifetime.

But Susan didn't want a safety-net. She tried hard not to think about what she really wanted – that hurt too much – but it was something that no amount of money could buy.

But she could afford a car. It was her first term at college and she hadn't many friends yet, but the car made friends, even if some of her year were plainly envious. They didn't know about the money, and she

110

didn't tell them because she didn't want anyone to know. Sometimes she pretended she didn't know herself, because knowing hurt.

The car was small and silver; 'Quicksilver' she christened it. The man at the garage seemed sceptical that Susan, who looked young for her age, could just walk in and buy a new car, but Mr Graf must have reassured him because when she went to collect Quicksilver the man fell over himself explaining the controls and telling her which switch washed the windows, or turned on the heating, or extended the aerial.

The first minutes of driving on her own were like diving off the top board. Then after the first traffic lights and the first right-hand turn Susan relaxed and switched on the radio. She could manage the gears, the brakes responded instantly; the only drawback was the stop-start traffic. It took almost as long to get out of the suburbs with their identical shopping parades and unsmiling houses as it did to reach Gran's cheerful cottage once she got onto the motorway. Then she flew. The car zipped along, gulping down the miles, breathing a little more heavily uphill and then swooping down so that the air gusted through the window, towsling Susan's hair.

It was best at night, when there was less traffic and she felt slightly frightened. Like watching the late-night movie on TV when the others were out. Gran was anxious about her being out late; what would she do if the car broke down? Susan replied that it was a new car and why should it go wrong? And it wasn't as though she was driving across the Sahara.

'Gran, there are telephones, even on the motorway. I got a subscription to the AA – and I expect someone would stop and help.'

'*That*'s what I'm afraid of,' Gran said. 'You can't be too careful these days. There are some awful people about.'

'It won't happen,' Susan said reassuringly. 'Honestly,

Gran, if I listened to you I'd never do anything.' And she put the idea of a breakdown firmly out of her mind. Or at least on the fringe of it. There *was* danger at night – why even a brightly lit petrol station could seem menacing if a gang of youths spilled out of an old car or roared in on motorbikes. She did wonder what she'd do if there was a holdup. Nothing brave, for sure.

Quicksilver made her popular. You could pack so much gear in it and not have to worry about the late-night buses. Only one other person in her year had a car, and nobody believed that Joe's old wreck had really passed its MOT.

Susan told her flatmates that Quicksilver was a present from a rich uncle – and if there were remarks about it must be nice to have rich relatives, they did at least believe that she was as hard up as everyone else. No one admitted to being well off. She didn't say anything about the safety-net, and one night when they were all talking about parents, she said that hers were in South America and had left her behind with Gran because they didn't want to upset her exams.

'Have you been out to see them?' asked Glenys.

'N-No. I hate flying, and it would take too long to get there any other way.' That at least was true.

'How awful! Being cut off from your family.' Glenys's best friend was her sister and she was always going home for the weekend.

And then, mercifully, Alex started talking about Rag Week.

Susan didn't go back to Gran at weekends because there was so much going on at college. She'd joined the drama group and had a tiny part – not much more than a walk-on – in the Christmas production. It didn't take long to rehearse, but she enjoyed hanging around with the theatre set. First-years were expected to know their place, and this suited Susan. She didn't want to play the lead; she preferred sitting in a corner watching Roger Tringham do his big scene and wondering whether by next year she might possibly be good enough and bold enough to act with him. Once, when he'd forgotten his script, she'd lent him hers – and was rewarded with a brief smile. She'd spent the rest of Saturday walking on air. He didn't return it, so that she had to buy another one, but it didn't matter. She would willingly have sacrificed her copy every rehearsal.

One Friday in the middle of November on the spur of the moment she decided to visit Gran. It would be a surprise for her, and if Gran wasn't expecting Susan she wouldn't be able to watch the clock and imagine the worst. Certainly if she rang up Gran would be sure to say, 'Why not come tomorrow, in the daylight?'

By the time she started out, it wasn't an ideal night for driving. It was late in the year for sunshine, and all day its golden glow had been hazy and diluted. At twilight the mist began to close in, blanketing the fields and thickening into fog. The streets around the college were smudged and dingier than usual, and there were few people about. Chippies and petrol stations flared in the sullen gloom, and as Susan oustripped them and came to the final limit of the suburbs the houses seemed to huddle together, collars turned up, hands in pockets of fog. She shivered and switched on the heater, though normally she disliked its suffocating warmth.

Now there were long gaps between the houses and a confusion of signs heralded the latest extension to the motorway. A stretch of woodland yawned with empty sockets where trees had been uprooted and tossed aside as though by some careless giant; a string of red and white bollards attempted to outline the road. Susan slowed down. It wasn't at all clear which was the way ahead and which blind alleys ending in silent machinery. Fog wound itself round the car like a bandage, sealing Susan in. She wasn't sure whether she was driving in the middle of the road – or even on the right side.

She inched the car forward. Its lights bounced unhelpfully back from the blank wall that loomed only a few feet from the bonnet; the wipers seemed to have developed a nervous tic as they strove to give the windscreen a segment of clarity.

Susan felt vulnerable. She had promised Gran that she would never pick up hitchhikers, but if there were any on such a night they would have no difficulty in picking her up. She was travelling at walking pace, and a determined man or woman could easily wrench open the door. Hadn't there been something on the radio about an escaped prisoner loose in the area? What price Gran's fears if she were to be found ... or worse, not found ...

It's the same road you've driven along heaps of times, she told herself. Just because it's hidden by a bit of fog doesn't mean it's not there. Try and remember what you usually pass round here.

She had not yet reached the Motorway sign and before it there were some houses that were boarded up and due for demolition. They might just be visible, but not the vast PYO farm that promised strawberries, podded peas and husks of sweet corn in summer, or the nursery with acres of greenhouses and a Gnomes Park. Peter had wanted one as a joke the time they bought some rose bushes for Mum's birthday.

Why had she suddenly remembered that? She must never, never let herself think about Mum and Dad and Peter.

She had expected the roundabout to be lit up, but when at last the road seemed to bear left she could only sense the great circle on her right. The motorway should be the third spoke. Susan counted out loud to reassure herself as she moved forward into a blankness that retreated before her headlights. Somewhere must be the other half of the carriageway, but she could hear and see nothing. Irritatingly her watch seemed to have stopped, and she had no idea how long she had been crawling forward before the fog began to dissolve and the speedometer needle flickered upward. She changed gear as the car picked up speed, twenty-five, thirty, seeming alarmingly fast.

A string of cat's eyes glared accusingly up at her and she saw that she was straddling the middle of the road. She pulled over hastily and then stopped. Where on earth was she? Plainly not on the motorway, and possibly not even heading in the right direction. Yet there was something familiar about the road. It curved uphill, and Susan felt she knew what was at the top. Her foot jerked down on the accelerator and the car roared up the hill. Just before the summit there was a small road sign with the words 'Death Hill'.

The chill Susan felt had nothing to do with the name itself, unpleasant though it was. 'Death Hill' had been a landmark on the way home. Dad had explained that it referred to a nearby motor racing track that had a deadly bend at this point and not to their road, but he was surprised the authorities hadn't changed it since the name did give one a nasty turn. The road Susan was on was the road home, though the last time she'd been on it she'd been far too young to drive. Dad had been driving and they'd all been together, she and Mum and Peter.

At least she wasn't lost, for not only was the road an indelible part of her childhood but it was also the road to Gran's cottage. She went on the motorway now because it was quicker, and because she didn't want to drive past the house they had lived in – before the accident.

It had happened so quickly. One minute they were going on holiday and had just taken their seats in the plane and fastened their seat-belts. There was a pretty stewardess who helped Susan change places with Peter because he wanted to see out of the window. It had saved her life. The plane had just begun to move when there was a bump followed by smoke and confusion.

She didn't want to remember what had happened to Mum and Dad and Peter. She couldn't see them through the smoke; couldn't hear them through the uproar. Someone had grabbed her arm and thrust her down the aisle, and the stampede had carried her forward and thrown her out of the plane, her lungs singed and barely able to cope with the life-saving fresh air. Later they had told her, gently, that Mum and Dad and Peter had not been so lucky. They were gone, extinguished, and it hurt all the more because she hadn't said goodbye to them. It didn't seem possible that death could be like that: so sudden, so irreversible. If she'd known, she'd have been much nicer that last half hour, instead of bickering with Peter and being irritable to Mum. She loved them, but she often wondered if they had realised that, or had gone into the darkness with only the memory of her bad temper ...

There'd been lots of sympathy and people she didn't know talking in hushed voices – which she hated – and she'd been glad to start a new life at a new school while living with Gran. The only way she could cope was by forgetting, forgetting that she had ever had a family, by pretending that they had gone to South America. At first Gran had tried to talk about Mum and Dad, but when Susan didn't reply and she saw her deliberately expressionless face, she accepted that Susan had to shut them out. If only she would cry, she thought, it would help her to come to terms with her grief. But Susan didn't cry.

It was vital, she had realised, not to let them slip back, though they lay in wait all around her. The past was a minefield of memories, and even when she had put away the photographs and avoided the places they went to and the things they used to do, they would steal back – on birthdays and at Christmas; when she came top in English and Dad would have been so pleased; on Saturday afternoons when she saw other families together ...

The car reached the top of the hill and everything was as Susan remembered it. It was some miles from the nearest town and yet not a proper village. There was the Olde Barn Restaurant where they had posh barbecues, Mr Woods's garage and a couple of pubs. And there was the stop where she and Peter had waited for the school bus; the house with the orchard where they'd sneaked in to pinch apples; the field where the Armstrongs had kept a smelly goat and an overweight pony; and the muddy lane which led to the brook, that was fun to squelch down in wellies ...

Her childhood came flooding back ... But for those few minutes in the plane they might still be living here, her parents waiting up for her, looking forward to hearing about college. She was jerked back into the present as the car swerved and then bumped alarmingly. It felt as though someone was trying to wrest the steering wheel from her, and she fought to regain control of Quicksilver and bring it to a halt. She sat for a few seconds, her heart racing, before she felt able to get out of the car and see what had happened.

She hadn't run over anything – her first fear – but the back wheel nearest the kerb sagged ominously: a puncture.

Susan felt helpless. The salesman had pointed out the kit for changing a wheel, but getting out the spare wasn't easy and she doubted whether she would be able to unscrew the nuts.

The road was deserted; nothing had passed either way since she had emerged from the fog. It was a night for being in front of the fire or perhaps, since it must be late, in bed. Susan shivered. There was, she remembered, a phone box at the far end of the houses and the sensible thing to do – the only thing to do – was to phone the AA or the police. At least there were a few streetlights on this stretch of the road.

She switched on her warning lights and locked the car door. Quicksilver was flashing its distress signal as

Susan gave an extra twist to her college scarf and told herself not to run. Time for that if anyone appeared; but there was no one about. She would have to walk past their old house, and she wondered who lived there now. The arrangements had been taken care of by lawyers and her grandmother had spared her the details, only explaining that her father had taken out life insurance and the airline was paying compensation, so that one day she would inherit a lot of money. Susan had just begun to realise that the money had the power to change her life as surely as her parents' death had done.

Some of the houses were in darkness, but she saw there were lights in their house. Her mother had always left the porch light on when her father was late home and the new owners must feel the same, for the light shone out as she remembered it. She had the feeling – ridiculous though it was – that were she to walk up the path and look through the window they would still be there: Dad watching the box and Mum trying to read or do her knitting while Peter ... Peter, if he was still the same age as when it had happened, would be in bed. Unless they all still existed somewhere ... so that Peter had gone on growing, like her. Would she ever be able to accept that their lives had come to a full stop, that they were not in South America or anywhere else, but non-existent except in her memory?

Suddenly she was aware that there was someone behind her. Perhaps the man – for she was instantly sure that it was a man – had been there some time without her noticing. But now he was visible and scurrying towards her. What was he doing out? she wondered. Even without fog it was hardly the night for a walk and no bus had passed either way, so he couldn't be some innocent passenger completing the last few yards of his journey home.

All Gran's fears and warnings raced through Susan's mind. 'Never go out alone at night. Never go anywhere lonely. Be suspicious of a man on his own. Terrible things happen these days ... it's all the fault of television ... ' She took Gran with a large pinch of salt but supposing she was right ...

It would be a mistake to run but Susan began to walk faster. She sensed that he was walking faster too – and gaining on her. It was such an ordinary, innocent stretch of road in daylight: the houses set back from the pavement with long narrow lawns shielded by bushes and hedges. Would anyone hear if she screamed? Mr Woods's garage, much grander than she remembered it, was closed. The Flying Horse might still be open, but it was beyond the last house and she doubted whether she could reach it in time.

She was nearly level with her old home when she looked back again. The man was now only a streetlight away; it showed him as a burly figure in an anorak. Susan's heart was pounding. She must get help before it was too late. The light in the front room gave the drawn curtains their familiar warm glow as she pushed open the gate and ran up the path. She rang the bell and then as the figure paused at the gate hammered on the door.

'Mum, Dad, come quickly! Help me!' She was so desperate that she uttered the first words that came into her head.

Why didn't they come! She knew they were there, behind the curtains' apricot glow. Her mother and father would always be there, caring about what happened to her, ready to help.

There was movement inside the house. Someone was coming to the door, but the man was coming up the path.

Susan banged louder, hoping that the noise would frighten him off. She realised that she was trapped between the man and whoever was about to open the door, and with all her might she willed it to be Mum or Dad. But then as Mum opened the door, it came to her beyond all shadow of doubt that although they still loved her as much as she loved them, Mum and Dad were DEAD ...

Her heart seemed to stop beating and she fell forward on to the doorstep.

'What's going on?' a woman's voice asked as she looked down at the body on the step and across at her husband.

'You tell me,' he replied. 'I was walking along behind a girl when suddenly for no apparent reason she ran up the path and starting banging on our door.'

They bent down over Susan, and when she opened her eyes she saw the concerned faces of two complete strangers. She began to cry, and at last the tears were for Mum and Dad and Peter.

THE OTHER SIDE OF DARK

JOAN LOWERY NIXON

When Stacy McAdams wakes in a hospital room to discover she has been in a coma for the past four years, her problems are only just beginning.

An innocent thirteen-year-old trapped in the body of a mature seventeen-year-old, Stacy has a lot of catching up to do. She yearns for the familiarity of her previous world.

Stacy is heartbroken to discover that her mother has been killed. Murdered by the same stranger who shot Stacy four years ago – and she is the only eye-witness. The only eye-witness to a murderer who hasn't been caught . . .

LIGHTNING

COLD FEET

JEAN RICHARDSON

I turned to look back, and saw that the big old farmhouse building was gone, and that all that was left was the low shape of a cottage or hut, no bigger than one of our barns. But there wasn't time to think about that. Water was lapping round my bare feet. I heard a massive creaking and could just make out the shape of an enormous bulk moving, the hull, masts and all, and riggings, and straining sails, of a galleon.

There was the cry again. This time I knew even before the light came up again what it was. A child was in the water, and he was shouting for help.

Haunting tales to thrill and chill from Robert Westall, Joan Aiken, Antonia Barber, Philip Pullman, Pamela Oldfield, Alison Prince, Jean Richardson and Berlie Doherty.

'Most distinguished,'
The Times Educational Supplement

LIGHTNING